Author of Cynthia

Lemuel

The Romance of Politics: Vol.I.

Author of Cynthia

Lemuel
The Romance of Politics: Vol.I.

ISBN/EAN: 9783337124274

Printed in Europe, USA, Canada, Australia, Japan

Cover: Foto ©Andreas Hilbeck / pixelio.de

More available books at **www.hansebooks.com**

L E M U E L

The Romance of Politics.

BY

THE AUTHOR OF 'CYNTHIA.'

' O Vita, misero longa felici brevis ! '—PUBLIUS.

IN TWO VOLUMES.

VOL. I.

LONDON: TINSLEY BROTHERS,
8 CATHERINE STREET, STRAND, W.C.

1 8 8 3.

COLSTON AND SON, PRINTERS, EDINBURGH.

LEMUEL.

CHAPTER I.

IT is not a question of instinct, mother, or of inheritance : I know nothing of the instinct of race, and I acknowledge no country. All I know is that I am. I gaze around me, and wonder whence I came; I look into the past for my origin, I peer into the future for my destiny — I have discovered neither. All I know is, as I have said, that I am. The confession is humiliating, but I can see no means of escape from it, and no man, it seems, can suggest any. It is idle to talk to me of faith; what you call faith is revolt—only a passionate protest against death. I love our old Hebrew psalmody—the songs of our people, those sighs of ages; but I have no faith in them. · They were the first sounds I distinctly remember to have heard, and they will be dear to me all my days, for they came from your own lips, mother, as you rocked me to rest in my baby-cot. It may be they will be the last sounds that I shall hear upon earth, at any rate the last that I shall care to hear; but, I repeat, I have no longer any faith in them. In short, I am an unbeliever.

Lemuel Leverson had been pacing

backwards and forwards as he delivered himself of these sentiments. His mother sat by the fireside and did not interrupt him. At length he came to an end; but, not receiving any response, he looked up and saw that his mother was weeping. Lemuel was an affectionate son, he loved his mother tenderly, he worshipped her with a genuine worship that to some extent filled the unnatural void caused by his loss of faith in God, and it was the very intensity of this affection, perhaps, that prepared the way and made it possible for him to ignore the existence of any higher claim upon his reverence and love.

Lemuel was by his mother's side instantly, and he kissed her forehead with tenderness.

'Should I not be honest, mother? You would not have me deceive you? You have taught me ever to say the truth as I hold it : surely it would be unworthy of you and of myself were I to feign that which I have ceased to feel?

But Lemuel's mother was not to be consoled. She had brought up her son from infancy in the strict observance of the law of Israel, in which she had herself walked all her days ; she would have seen him dead at her feet as willingly as that he should become an outcast from her people.

' " From the morning watch even until night," she murmured, " let Israel hope in the Lord " !—My son, oh, my son !'

Lemuel Leverson was the only son of

his mother. He had completed twenty summers, and had outstripped most young men of his age in knowledge and intelligence. And it was these first victories that had filled his heart with pride, that enabled him to stand unabashed in his mother's presence and to proclaim his infidelity. He believed he was not as other men. The prosaic men around him were not his equals, assuredly; and, strong in this belief, he did not hesitate to undertake the solution of the deepest questions, and to rush to conclusions at which other men hardly arrive at the end of laborious lives.

From his father, who had been dead some years, Lemuel Leverson had inherited but a moderate fortune, and the time had now arrived when the perennial question had to be answered, what was Mrs Leverson to do with her son? It is the question of questions for every parent at this stage, and it is alarming to think how much depends upon the answer. But for Mrs Leverson there was really no choice. Her son was not of an ordinary stamp that would be counselled; he did not wait for, much less court, the advice of uncle or aunt, or cautious attorney. Away with them; he would have none of them. Lemuel would choose his own destiny; he would dispose of himself and of his fortunes. In the pride of his intellect he was at war already with the world that surrounded him, and he would not be advised by his enemies. He felt that he possessed within himself an energy, a vitality, superior to any they had ever known. Why, then, was his course in life to be limited and bounded by the narrow views of these pigmies, to be mapped out and measured with stake and line by these trembling hands?

They approached him at first with the easy confidence of superiority with which ordinary youth, just let loose from school, inspires men and women of the world. It was ingenuous youth that had to be treated: why was it not to be moulded after the fancy of the elders? They laid hands upon him and turned him round, and regarded his points, much as they of the turf do a colt of uncertain pedigree, but their judgment was delivered in doubtful whispers, for it was perceived that there was a tendency to jib, which augured no good in the opinion of the experts. There were indications of temper too, over which they shook their heads and muttered wise saws, but their worst anticipations were more than realised when, upon one advising law and another physic, Lemuel, starting to his feet, consigned them all to perdition with an oath.

The uncle and the aunt and the cautious attorney were aghast. There was but one sentiment among them all.

' He will be a sad trial to his mother !' they exclaimed, as they left the house in company. ' It is a thousand pities, and with so fair a prospect in the world !'

' Dear me !' quoth the attorney, ' I have no patience with· such folly. The law provides such pickings, too, for a man

with a good connection—such snug berths!
Dear me! dear me!'

'He is a most ill-conditioned young
man,' averred Uncle Leverson; 'a child
of wrath, I apprehend, and an affliction to
his family.'

'He might as well be a Christian,'
muttered Aunt Tabitha Cohen, as she
passed out between the uncle and the
attorney.

'Dear me! dear me!' all three exclaimed in chorus, as they shook the dust
from their feet and took their departure
in haste. What further room was there
indeed for the intervention of sage
counsels? The trusted advisers of the
family had been driven forth one and all
with contumely, and their gloomy counte-
nances sufficiently informed Mrs Leverson

that her worst forebodings had been realised, and that her son's strange temper
had asserted itself once more in the ungo-
vernable form to which she had of late
become accustomed. Mrs Leverson sat
by her fireside and wept afresh. She
rocked herself to and fro in her great
oaken seat, and mourned over the wil-
fulness of her child.

But Lemuel was not moved to peni-
tence. He was even further emboldened
by this victory, for he felt that he had
taken his destiny into his own hands
irrevocably now, and he must bear himself worthy of the responsibility. He
was even angry with his mother when
he beheld her tears; for it was a
powerful hold upon him still the love
that he bore her; it was the one bar-

rier that stood between him and entire emancipation. If his mother would only leave him to himself, and acquiesce in his judgment of what should be his career in life, Lemuel thought that he could almost be happy.

'It is my ambition to be great,' he exclaimed. 'I cannot stoop to an every-day employment. I feel that I possess within me the power to become famous : who shall say to me, "Be an attorney's clerk or a hospital drudge?" I feel as Samuel must have felt. True, he was a mystic from the beginning, and an ardent believer; but his was a grand life.'

Lemuel had approached the window, which was half open, and was now gazing intently on the blue summer sky.

'I wish I could believe like Samuel,' he continued. 'I feel I should be capable of great works. Belief in some great principle is essential to success in life; of that I am convinced. There can be no success worthy the name without enthusiasm; there can be no enthusiasm without such a belief. Samuel believed in God and was great; he judged Israel all the days of his life. I cannot believe like Samuel, indeed, but I also have a faith that may yet accomplish much. I believe in myself. Yes; I have had it in my heart of hearts from the first, and have scarce understood it till now; but it is a faith as deep as that of Israel, as enthusiastic as that of Mahomet. It was the faith of the conquerors of the world. It was the faith of Arbela, and of the Rubicon, and of Marengo. Yes; I recognise it now; henceforth it is mine; I embrace it from this hour.'

'Why, you young jackanapes!' exclaimed Lemuel's uncle, who, having returned by invitation to dine with his sister-in-law, had overheard the conclusion of this soliloquy, 'you are not yet of age, and you imagine that you are a philosopher already! Pah!'

Another might have been startled by this unlooked-for interruption of his reverie; but Lemuel turned round slowly and with deliberation towards his uncle, regarding him with a gaze of impassive indifference.

'Age is not always to be counted by years,' observed Lemuel; 'and that the understanding of a man is grey hairs is among the wise sayings of our people. I am, moreover, of the poet's mind that—

"In hoary youth Methusalems may die." '

'It had been well for you,' answered Jacob Leverson with warmth, 'had you studied the sayings of our people more and the poets less. You might then have learnt, perhaps, that there is a "whip for a horse, and a snaffle for an ass, and a rod for the back of fools." '

'We two sha'n't agree long,' said Lemuel calmly; 'suppose we separate?'

'With all my heart,' said Lemuel's uncle; 'you can go where you please. As for me, I have no desire to expose myself to further insult.'

'Then my mother and I dine alone to-day,' remarked Lemuel as he threw up the window and walked out upon the terrace.

'The young man will be a thorn in his mother's side all her days,' thought Jacob Leverson as he left the house. 'Indeed, her lot is not to be envied with such a son. The man that considers himself a born genius is, generally speaking, a born fool; that has been my experience, and I can see no reason to make an exception in favour of my nephew. Dear me! Dear me!'

Lemuel having disposed of his uncle and routed his aunt, fell into a fit of melancholy. The victory had in truth been too easy. Where was the glory of the fight? Triumphs such as these are of small account. Only the first blow has been struck, and the blood is scarce stirred when the struggle is at an end and the enemy in retreat. Men of this stamp are the least satisfactory of foes; men who are ever on the look-out for an excuse to fly and save their own honour without adding to yours. But the hot blood of youth soon asserted itself; and the disenchantment which had followed the first hour of freedom passed quickly away. Lemuel was himself again; the same dreaming, enthusiastic boy that he had ever been. His spirits rose as the vision of the future appeared before him; his fervid imagination came to his aid once more; the consciousness of power returned, and he longed for the opportunity to measure himself with the reputed wits and politicians of the world. Hitherto he had contemplated them from afar off, or had studied them in books only. They were not within striking distance; but Lemuel had discovered nothing in their aspect to daunt or to discourage him. On the contrary, their littlenesses appeared at every turn, and there were chinks and flaws visible in their armour, through which one that was skilled in the use of the sword or the poignard might deal deadly thrusts. To rise to eminence was his ambition, and every man that succeeds has to beat down the world first unless his ancestors have done it for him. The fierce fight happens once at least in the history of every family that rises to fame; in most it has to be renewed again and again; but, once Fame's trumpet has proclaimed your triumph, it will echo through all ages.

To place himself on an equality with the world for the battle of life it was essential that Lemuel should mingle with society and study mankind at close quarters. And on this object his mind was now set. Mrs Leverson would have kept her son by her side ; for her there was no joy when he was absent ; but his indomitable will asserted itself irresistibly. Expeditions from home were not now simply proposed as of old ; they were decided in the same instant, and it was no longer for his mother to advise, but only to inquire the day and the hour. She knew from experience that remonstrance was idle, for Lemuel never changed his mind —it was one of his theories. His mother contented herself with rocking to and fro by the fireside and shedding tears in silence.

CHAPTER II.

FROM the time of her husband's death Mrs Leverson had mingled but little in the world. She continued to reside in the pretty villa in the northern suburbs of London, where also she had passed most of her married life. The house was not a large one, and Mrs Leverson had no ambition to occupy a more pretentious dwelling. The neighbourhood was inhabited by homely people. They were mostly engaged in business or but recently retired from it, for there was little that could be called aristocratic in that district. Mrs Leverson had but few friends among them, nor did she seek to extend her acquaintance. For her the society of her son was all-sufficient, and since his return from school he had been but rarely absent from her side. And on his part Lemuel was even more reserved than his mother. He felt as if, he had dropped from the clouds into the midst of these people, so completely was he a stranger amongst them, to so great a distance was he removed from their ways of regarding life. The petty interests that absorbed their thoughts habitually he looked upon as children's toys, and the fears that followed on trifles in their minds were to him as the alarms of the serving girl whose highest idea of a catastrophe is limited to the shivering of a potsherd. He was above and beyond them immeasurably, and his best companionship he ever found to be his own.

One great house there was surrounded by a stately park where at intervals resided the lord of the manor; but the dwellers around saw little of him. Once a year in the warm summer weather there would be a *fête* at the Manor House that attracted a brilliant throng from the West End, after which all would subside again into its wonted peace and solitude. It was a delightful spot situate on the northern heights, and the park that surrounded the mansion embraced hill and dale and soft undulating meadows, that rested the eye weary from the glare of the streets. A miniature lake slept in the valley, and from its margin rose a hanging wood of beech and dark cedars wherein the heron made its nest. To all appearance the town might have been miles away, so secluded was the place.

In the distance beneath, stretching away as far as eye could follow, lay the great city. And through the long avenues of pines' that crowned the ridges in the park there was a vista of towering monuments, and spires that sought the skies, that struggled, as it were, with the mist and fume to penetrate to the upper and clearer air, types of human aspiration still striving for something nobler and better than is to be found by the earth's surface.

Hither as the evening closed came

the soft clamour of distant bells, and lights commenced to twinkle from afar through the gloom as the great human family gathered round their firesides when the day's labour was ended. And here many a time would Lemuel wander amid the groves, losing himself in day dreams in their shadowy glades, or resting beneath the solemn cedars while his brooding spirit wrestled with the unsolved problems of human existence, and his imagination was on fire with visions of the misty future. He felt that the time for action was at hand, that he stood even upon the threshold of manhood, and when he looked out upon the world with which he had to deal, the prospect, it seemed to him, was fair and inviting. And so is it ever to smiling youth. He may be on the brink of the precipice, the jaws of death may open ever so wide, but the sunshine of life is upon him, and its beauty is before and around him, and he is blind to the yawning chasm. And it is as it should be. Life has to be faced as it stands, be it for better or for worse, and the more hopefully and the more confidently a man commences his career, the more likely it is that he will conclude it successfully. There are two qualities in life that are the seeds of its heroes, audacity and discretion ; and in the happy blending of both are found its Cæsars and its Napoleons. The world recognises nature's masterpiece and goes on its knees.

There had been a great *fête* at the

manor ; and, as evening fell, the company began to disperse, and carriages laden with most that was noblest and fairest in London society were hastening down the steep incline that leads towards the city. Lemuel was returning to his home, and had commenced to ascend the hill, when of a sudden there was a cry, followed by a crash on the height above, and presently was to be seen a carriage coming at full speed down the incline, the horses galloping frantically, while the carriage swayed wildly from side to side. A servant had fallen from the box, and had just been raised from the ground insensible, but the coachman still held the reins, though he had evidently lost the control. Onward in its headlong course came the carriage down the hill, exposing

its occupants to destruction at every instant. These were seen to consist of two
ladies, the elder of whom had fallen back
in a fainting condition, whilst the terrified
cries of the younger added further horror
to the scene. Men turned pale and held
their breath as the horses, no longer re-
strained, swept by in their mad career,
and women felt sick with terror, and
averted their faces lest they should see the
end. At the bottom of the hill the road
took a sharp turn, and it was apparent
that if this point were reached, the carriage, would be dashed to pieces, and the
occupants would, in all probability, not
escape with their lives. The fatal turn
was close at hand, and the final catastrophe
appeared to be inevitable, when Lemuel,
rushing into the middle of the way, laid

hands upon the animal that was the nearest to him, and bringing his whole weight to bear, succeeded in forcing it to its knees. The carriage was brought to a stand on the instant, and, ere men had time to realise what had occurred, Lemuel was already gallantly assisting the occupants to alight. The elder of the ladies was no longer conscious of what had occurred, but the younger had still sufficient presence of mind to ask through her tears for the name of her deliverer. But Lemuel declined thanks; he had no desire for the acknowledgments of those whom he had rescued, though it were from all but certain death; to him what he had done was but a simple act of duty.

The incident had indeed almost passed from his memory, and he had ceased to think of it by the following morning, when a servant appeared at the gate of Mrs Leverson's villa, and presented the card of the Duchess of Shetland. This was accompanied by a message to the effect that the duchess would esteem it as a particular favour if Mr Leverson would call at Shetland House in the course of the day.

It was a noble mansion in which the duchess resided; one of the very few in London, the extent and proportions of which recall to the imagination the palaces of Italy. It was altogether worthy of the traditions of the great house of Shetland, and, on her part, the duchess had ever sustained the reputation of the family for splendid hospitality. Nor was it the magnificence of a season only, which is always somewhat forced,—it was the habitual grandeur that needs no effort and causes no strain. The duchess had reigned in society as one of its fairest and best ornaments in the days of the Regency, when the fair and the good seemed to form separate sections of the community. She had passed through the fire of a corrupt generation, and had come forth unscathed and unsullied, and now in her old age there was none that was more honoured or more courted than she. Possessed of great wealth she spent it lavishly, and at her house were to be met most of those who were highly distinguished by birth or by merit.

With the duchess resided her niece, Lady Muriel, the orphan child of the Earl of Bellecourt, the duchess's brother. To the duchess Lady Muriel had been as a daughter ; she was heiress of her father's vast estates, and it was understood that from the duchess also she would inherit a great fortune.

For the first time Lady Muriel had been presented to the world of London this year, and society had pronounced unhesitatingly its verdict in her favour. Her beauty was not, indeed, of the showy type ; she was the primrose that grows on the shady bank in all its native simplicity, not the gaudy carnation artificially trained to adorn the trim *parterre.* She sought not to dazzle ; for her admiration had no value, and she did not court flattery; her beauty did not depend upon any regularity of feature, it was the charm of her manner that first attracted attention, and the sweetness of her smile converted it into love. Lady

Muriel was, in fact, wholly unspoilt by the adulation of the world ; the simplicity and truthfulness of her character seemed to shield her effectually from its temptations.

It was midday when Lemuel presented himself at the portals of Shetland House. He was not abashed by the array of powdered footmen, or the doubtful glances cast at him by the groom of the chambers as he was conducted to the presence. Through chamber after chamber he followed ; rooms filled with all that can satisfy the eye, or add pleasure to existence ; walls that glowed with priceless works that had adorned at some time the salons of a French palace, or hung in the cloisters of an Italian monastery ; cabinets curious with rare china ; tables, precious in themselves, laden with the thousand objects adapted for pleasure or for use, that only the magic touch of woman can display to the best advantage.

Lemuel had not been accustomed to the luxury of palaces; he had seen none of their splendours before this day, but he held his head erect, nevertheless, until it was bowed with becoming modesty before the little old lady with the pale placid face and round blue eyes that sat propped up with pillows in the middle of the sofa.

No sooner had Lemuel's name been announced than the little old lady made an effort to rise, a mark of attention which she had been accustomed to display to royalty alone, and, holding forth her hand, signified to Lemuel to take his place by her side.

For a moment the duchess did not speak; she continued to hold Lemuel by the hand, gazing at him with her round blue eyes, and Lemuel, who was at a loss to understand at first, presently perceived that they were filled with tears. When she found words the duchess was not slow to convey her sense of gratitude and admiration. She thanked Lemuel warmly for his gallant act ; nor was he permitted to depart until he had promised to return to dine on the following day.

' For my niece,' the duchess explained, ' whose gratitude you have earned, not less than my own, is too ill and nervous to-day to leave her room, but she will, I trust, be recovered sufficiently by to-morrow to thank you in person.'

When Lemuel found himself again in the street, it appeared to him as if, in these four-and-twenty hours, he had been making an excursion into fairyland, into those enchanted bowers where we have read that good fairies smile upon you, and take you under their protection, and make life bright and joyous of a sudden, and full of surprise and adventure. But it was no dream, it was no fairy tale, it was all substantial enough—an opening in life that might be the means of changing his whole future had appeared before him; the slowly revolving wheel of fortune seemed to have taken a sudden turn, and to be spinning round upon its axle. The dreams of success in the great world that Lemuel had dreamt beneath the cool shade of the cedars might be realised, he thought, even now, and in a way the most unexpected, and he bounded along with elastic step, and a faith in himself that was more firm than ever.

It was an evening towards the end of June, and the windows of Shetland House, that looked upon the terrace, were thrown widely open ; the air was soft and balmy, and the fresh fragrance of flowers from conservatory and garden pervaded the spacious and dimly-lighted saloons. The duchess had just entered the reception-room as the first guests were announced, and she was still engaged in adjusting her delicately-embroidered and scented gloves.

'Mr Lemuel Leverson, your grace,' vociferated the groom of the chambers.

The duchess advanced to meet Lemuel, and, welcoming him warmly, presented him to her niece, Lady Muriel Bellecourt.

The young lady blushed deeply as she offered her hand, and in the sweetest confusion imaginable, endeavoured to

make her expressions of gratitude intel-
ligible. It did not matter greatly, indeed,
whether Lady Muriel succeeded in making
clear her meaning in words; for there
was that to be read in her eyes which
was more eloquent than many speeches.
But in another instant the announcement
of the arrival of a royal duchess called
her away. At dinner Lady Muriel was
placed at some distance from Lemuel;
but, at every pause in the conversation,
her eyes were found wandering in the
same direction. There was, in fact, only
one thought that occupied her mind;
it seemed to her that every noble
and chivalrous quality was stamped in
Lemuel's face. She felt something more
than the debt of gratitude that was his
due; she recognised in him an influence

such as women are not fashioned to resist, a power and force of character before which it only remains to fall down and worship. It is, perhaps, what in the world is termed love at first sight, though its full meaning may not be recognised on either side at first. It may be in the man, or it may be in the woman; it is not usually in both. As a rule, one or the other has to be attracted and led. But if both are struck together, not all the powers of earth shall keep them asunder. Heaven has decreed it : stand off, ye potentates of clay !

As for Lemuel, the grace and sweetness of Lady Muriel filled him with admiration ; but it had not occurred to him to indulge in any more tender feeling. It appeared as if the barrier between himself and one

so highly placed were indeed insurmount-
able, and the very suggestion of love was
cast under foot and trampled upon. Even
the soft glances of those azure eyes that
fell upon him, each with a spell of its own
more potent than its predecessors, did not
disturb his habitual serenity. Lemuel was
not emotional; he was what the world
terms cold; but, with some men, the
world is thoroughly mistaken. It is not
always insensibility, nor is it indifference :
it may be refinement; it may be fastidi-
ousness that sways both the intellect and
the heart.

Such men detect alloy where ordinary
mortals are wont to discern only fine
gold; but when they do come upon the
pure and the perfect—for once only in a
lifetime, it may be—they are apt to be

carried away by a passion more headlong, more heedless a thousandfold, than
all the loves of the impressionable put
together. It was thus with Lemuel Leverson, but there was in addition the severe
discipline of reason that controlled passion and sentiment alike ; they were the
servants and helpmates of his reason,
never its master. They played the parts
assigned to them in the drama, but no
exaggerations were permitted ; they were
never suffered to go beyond the text ; and
it was not until the word was given that
wild passion and all-subduing love might
break away from their bonds with resistless energy.

CHAPTER III.

IT was an afternoon in the early part of July, and the London season was at its height. It had been a busy week for the world of fashion, and men and women were glad to escape, if only for a few hours, from the heat and the turmoil of the streets to breathe the purer air of some suburban retreat. And of these none possesses greater fascination for the weary and the overworked than Richmond.

It was the Sheen of our ancestors, who,

in thus naming it, gave expression to their sense of its singular beauty ; and so it remained until it became the favourite retreat of the Tudor princes. Here Henry the Seventh was wont to seek rest from the cares of State, and, in conferring upon the place a title by which he had himself been known in his youth, connected Richmond for ever in his mind with those happier days ere ambition made him a king and circumstances a tyrant.

Hither hastened his relentless son to await the echoes of the Tower guns, that told how the head of hapless Anne had fallen on the block. To Richmond came Elizabeth unwillingly to die, scared in those last days by the spectres of the scaffold that haunted her imagination, seeking such peace as she might in the sylvan solitudes of her palace at Richmond. Undefiled by foreign invasion or domestic turmoil, every tradition of the place is of rest, and its amenities are undisturbed by any memory of conflict.

Lemuel Leverson was leaning on the balustrade of the garden of the famous hotel on Richmond Hill, and gazing thence on the glorious prospect that stretches away until earth and heaven seem to unite in the blue distance. There was the winding stream, now vanishing, now re-appearing, taking its ease, as it were, amid the rich meadows and the soft woods of the Thames valley; nearer, at the foot of the terrace, where the honeysuckle yet grows untended and the wild clematis, the children romped and crowned themselves with flowers, and held hands and frolicked, and laughter was in their bright faces when they were noticed. The fountains played, and the garden was trim and gay with the summer roses as an Eastern princess decked in her jewels; and here and there sauntered or sat happy couples escaped from the sultry atmosphere of the town, enjoying the cool evening breeze for the half-hour before dinner was announced.

'I think you must have known my brother,' said Marcia Mowbray, a good-looking, fashionably-dressed woman, whose acquaintance Lemuel had formed at the Duchess of Shetland's party. 'Was he not at school with you?'

Lemuel made no reply. He gazed at Mrs Mowbray inquiringly, and with a puzzled expression.

'Oh, I had forgotten!' she exclaimed,

laughing; 'I have not told you what was my maiden name—how very dull of me! It was Lambton.'

'Lambton?' repeated Lemuel. 'And are you sister of Willie Lambton who was with me at Harrow?'

'He is my youngest brother,' said Marcia Mowbray. 'I had heard so much of you from Willie, that when I saw you and your name was mentioned, I could not doubt of your identity. I feel that I have known you for years, although we have only met so recently.'

'And so Willie spoke much to you of me,' said Lemuel. 'I wonder what it was that he told you?'

'He raved about you at one time,' said Marcia; 'even his holidays were a weariness to him, because of the loss of your companionship, then all at once he ceased to speak of you. Something had occurred, I am sure, but what it was he never confided to me. I often asked my brother, but he always evaded the question. Willie is very religious, you know,' Marcia Mowbray added, 'and I used to think that, perhaps, he had taken a prejudice against persons who professed your faith.'

'It was not that,' said Lemuel, slowly; 'no, it was not that; it was, if you must know, because I had none.'

'You had none! Surely you do not mean to say that you have no belief?'

'Not in the supernatural order,' replied Lemuel; 'in the order of nature my belief is that of a fanatic.'

Marcia Mowbray was not herself a devotee by any means, but she professed as much religion as the majority of her neighbours, and quite sufficient to satisfy the requirements of even the more staid portion of society. Her religion was not, indeed, suffered to interfere with her pursuits, but neither was it altogether shadowy. Religion had with her a general, not particular application, and her belief, without pretension to theological accuracy, was unquestioned, because it had never occurred to her to question it. It was a decided shock to find herself thus unexpectedly face to face with an avowed infidel. And the words were not, she knew, uttered flippantly. Lemuel looked older than he was, and he had spoken with deliberation.

'You have explained all now,' said Marcia Mowbray, 'and I am no longer at a loss to account for my brother's altered sentiments towards you. Pray, may I ask when it was that you commenced to repudiate religion ?'

'As soon as I began to reflect,' said Lemuel. 'Until the age of seventeen others thought for me; at eighteen I thought for myself; at nineteen I was what you would term an infidel.'

'You appear to have made astonishing progress when once you had begun,' continued Marcia Mowbray. 'Others have been more perplexed. To have thought out for oneself the problems of time and eternity, and to have arrived at a conclusion between seventeen and nineteen is a feat, believe me. Some men reputed wise have found a lifetime too short for the same purpose, I have heard.'

'It is very pleasant to believe,' said

Lemuel; 'it cheers the path of life, and smoothes the pillow in death. I was happier when I believed than I have since been; but I had no choice in the matter. I do not boast of my incredulity, neither do I affect to conceal it: those who are just to me say it is my misfortune, not my fault. Let me hope you will be of the number.'

'Then you would have me think that you are serious,' said Marcia, 'and I am sorry that it should be so; for I could have forgiven more readily a jest on such a subject than an attempted justification. But do not misunderstand me. I am not a theologian, and have no desire to argue the case. At present we are bent upon dining.'

It was at Marcia Mowbray's invitation

that Lemuel had joined the party at Richmond; and amongst the guests whose acquaintance he made there was Daphne Bland. She was a beautiful brunette of five-and-twenty, conscious of her good looks, and demonstrative to the point of danger. Her natural virtues were, in fact, so covered over by wanton worldliness as to be, even to the lynx-eyed, invisible, save in the case of the few that knew her intimately. Her husband she respected indeed, but failed altogether to obey. He was her senior by nearly forty years—a man of science and a philosopher, that loved best the recesses of his library. Yielding to the solicitations of her family, Daphne Dorrell had been persuaded to marry him after a stout resistance; but amongst the freaks of

our humanity, that of being buried alive
for choice has never been one, and
Daphne was not disposed to set the
example. In consenting to marry Ralph
Bland she had, she conceived, done her
duty to gods and men ; henceforth she determined that pleasure should have its turn.

At dinner Lemuel sat between Marcia
Mowbray and Daphne Bland. Each of
the women took an interest in Lemuel
from the first—Marcia, on account of
his singular character, and Daphne, for
his good looks. But in a contest for
the mastery, Marcia had the advantage ;
for ready wit, joined to audacity, will
generally carry the day, even if the victory
hang doubtfully for a space in the presence
of the god-like possession of beauty.

Daphne Bland was bold to rashness,

and at times she was betrayed by her feelings into wild flights of sentiment which, in the mouth of a married woman, are liable to be misconstrued. Hence the world judged her severely, and judged her rashly; but Daphne had also a sharp tongue, and the revilers got the worst of it for the most part.

'This is my first visit to Richmond,' remarked Lemuel. 'To you the place is doubtless familiar.'

'Why, yes,' answered Daphne. 'You see, my husband is fond of good food, and I have not much difficulty in inducing him to dine out. It is the least of my troubles. His consent once obtained, I make up a little party, and— *voilà tout.*'

'That is as it should be,' said Lemuel.

'The amenities of domestic life are assuredly among the most delightful of human experiences. I am convinced, moreover, that in these matters the wife should rule; and the husband is a wise man who respects her privilege.'

'Well, we need not discuss the question of my husband's wisdom,' said Daphne, with a shrill laugh; 'you do not know him, and so I should have an unfair advantage in the argument; but there are questions other than those connected with dining out, in which a wife may, without undue presumption, expect that her views will not be disregarded altogether.'

'Undoubtedly,' said Lemuel. 'But your cheery manner leaves little room for question that, in your case at least, the bounds of a wife's authority are extended rather than curtailed.'

'It is evident that you are not in the family secrets,' said Daphne. 'If you had been you would wonder at my venturing to smile at all. But, like the rest,' she added, with a sigh, 'you judge by appearances. Presently you will be told that I am frisky. Don't believe it. I am the saddest woman alive.'

'Incredible!'

'You see, my husband does not dance—,

'How strange!'

Daphne was somewhat startled by this remark, and scanned Lemuel's countenance narrowly. She apprehended that he was laughing at her.

'You are an amusing man,' she said at length in a tone of sarcasm. 'I can see that at a glance. But it might have been better had you waited until I had completed the sentence.'

Lemuel had, in fact, used the words almost mechanically. He had been observing Daphne with interest, and was amused at her volubility. He did not mean to offend her.

'Pardon the interruption,' he replied, 'I was listening attentively.'

'Well,' Daphne resumed, 'as I have said, my husband, not caring to dance at his age, will not suffer me to dance either. It is as nearly as possible unbearable.'

'Indeed!'

'You provoking creature! you know it is,' said Daphne, stamping her foot. 'Do you not dance?'

'Not of late years.'

'Of late years!' repeated Daphne.

'Pray, how many years have elapsed since you renounced the frivolities of youth ? '

' I have never had any.'

A peal of laughter was Daphne's response as the men rose from their seats to make way for the women to retire.

'You amuse me,' she said, looking back at Lemuel over her shoulder as she left the dining-room. 'You amuse me considerably. I must see you again.'

'What do you think of young Leverson?' said Marcia Mowbray, as she sauntered on the terrace with Daphne, after dinner.

'Oh, very young—a complete simpleton !' said Daphne; 'a veritable babe in the wood, I promise you. He danced years ago and has no frivolities. Delightful, is it not, in a youth of twenty? Between ourselves, he is a fool !'

'He may perhaps be a knave, and I fancy he is somewhat of a prig; but he is not a fool, believe me,' responded Marcia. 'He is a Hebrew by birth and an infidel by profession—'

'Good gracious! You are not serious?'

'But I am,' continued Marcia. 'There is no doubt on the subject. He made his profession of unbelief to me only this afternoon.'

'Then, what do you suppose he intended to convey by his silly remarks during dinner?' inquired Daphne, with some concern.

'Well,' replied Marcia, 'I think it was nothing more than an experiment on his part—I may say, a process of vivisection. He wanted to draw you out, and—don't be alarmed—to laugh at you. That was all.'

'To laugh at me! Perhaps you are right,' said Daphne, growing serious, 'and at one moment I suspected as much. I could kill him if I thought so—the coxcomb!'

'But, after all, it is difficult to feel really angry with a good-looking man,' Marcia observed, 'unless, indeed, you would con- found jealousy with anger. No; his worst faults are condoned when you look in his face; he has but to smile and you feel that you have already received compensation, and forgiven the offence.'

'Forgive him because he smiles upon you! Then you are easily pacified,' said Daphne. 'I am not by any means clear that it is wise to be thus forgiving. This readiness to pardon, this assurance of con- donation, encourages these good-looking men to be insolent beyond endurance.

Their impertinence knows no bounds at last, and you are fortunate if it does not culminate in the greatest crime of all—easy-going indifference.'

'That is maddening, I admit,' Marcia replied ; 'it is the unpardonable sin ; but my experience hitherto has not, I confess, led me to anticipate such a result.'

And now the men have rejoined the women on the terrace, and the party is about to separate. Lemuel raises his glass and searches for Daphne Bland in the twilight.

'Ah ! there she is,' he says to himself at length ; 'and a rare and precious specimen of the woman of society — caught on Richmond Hill, July the 5th, 1850. In she goes to my museum : she richly deserves a niche and a number.'

CHAPTER IV.

ARCIA MOWBRAY was the wife of the Right Hon. James Mowbray, Member of Parliament and Under Secretary of State. He was much engrossed in affairs, and few men connected with the administration were more industrious or more useful. He was a mighty master of detail, and engaged perpetually in the collection of facts; while to him the digestion of a blue-book was as keen an enjoyment, as exhilarating an exercise, as the chase to a Yorkshire squire. In finance he was esteemed an authority, his arithmetic was plausible and ingenious, but the fame of a financier is ephemeral, and excites no enthusiasm even if it be conspicuous. Finance touches the pockets of contemporaries, its benefits are personal and immediate for the most part, but even they who profit are rarely impressed, and posterity is seldom sensitive to the merits of departed financiers.

In private life the case is the same. It is well, indeed, to have had a thrifty progenitor in the family, but the chances are that some prodigal of the race will be pointed to as the more famous, even more creditable ancestor. Finance never yet made a hero nor statistics a statesman, and thus it happened that James Mowbray failed to create for himself a reputation commensurate with his efforts. He aspired to high office, but had made the mistake of constituting himself the drudge of the Cabinet. It was the bar that stood in the way of his advancement to the Supreme Council of the sovereign and the nation ; for his masters perceived that his usefulness would not survive the dignity.

Marcia Mowbray's ambition had been crowned with more success. It was the object and the occupation of her life to secure social distinction, and she had, in fact, achieved it by force of will and determination, despite many obstacles. For Marcia had a rough and ready manner that stood in the way of her popularity with the women, and she was plain spoken to an extent that gave offence to the men. She could be boisterous too on occasion, and at times she romped in a way that gave cause to the ribald to rail.

'I can't abide that woman,' Lady Millicent would remark over her breakfast-table—'she is so vulgar.'

But Marcia Mowbray was not vulgar, really; it was only Lady Millicent's way of putting it when she desired to avenge herself for Marcia's brusqueness the night before, coupled, it might be, with her own want of success in the ballroom.

But in dealing with society Marcia had a powerful lever to work with, and it enabled her to overcome many difficulties, for the Mowbrays had a fine house and made a great display, and herein was a cloak for a multitude of shortcomings. Marcia did not, it is true, make the best

use of these advantages, for she was
economical to a fault, and thus lost on
the one hand much that she had gained
on the other. Her dinners were sumptu-
ously served, but they were more often
réchauffés than *recherchés;* and those who
were asked to join her little parties to
Richmond were expected to pay their
share of the reckoning. She was profuse
in her invitations to the play, but here
again her parsimony prevailed, for they
who accompanied her contributed to the
evening's amusement by depositing the
price of their stalls ere they left. And
herein Marcia Mowbray blundered. En-
joyments that are paid for are only half
appreciated, and no man regards with
grateful glances the tax-gatherer of the
supper-table.

Marcia had an only daughter—Egidia —who had for ten years tempted to no purpose the golden youth of the ballrooms. Her blandishments had been vain, for, though men liked the girl, they were scared at her mother, and the trumpery tax scattered sentiment to the winds.

At Richmond, Egidia had scarcely exchanged a word with Lemuel. They had not been thrown together, but Lemuel had attracted her notice in a marked degree notwithstanding. There was a repose in his manner, a deep, steady gaze in his luminous dark eye that impressed her with a sense of power. Her curiosity was aroused ; there seemed to be so much hidden beneath that calm, unemotional exterior, much that might be either good or bad, interesting or commonplace, that Egidia longed to draw aside the veil and to know what he was really like ; for there is nothing that excites the female mind more than the placid, imperturbable gaze of a good-looking man : it is maddening, the women say. The pride that does not condescend in a woman's presence,. and is only scrupulously polite, brings her to her knees. It is man taking his place in nature, and forthwith woman assumes hers.

Egidia's eyes were henceforth often directed towards Lemuel's, and when they met she blushed involuntarily and turned away looking conscious. She felt that she could not hold her own with this man, young as he was, and without experience in the world ; she felt instinctively his inherent strength, and she knew from the first that she could be nothing more than a plaything in his hands. And it was much the same with the women all round. Even the anger of Daphne Bland told in Lemuel's favour, for Daphne was convinced now of his intellectual superiority, and she admired the man the more that she was vexed with herself.

The quiet reserve, the slightly cynical, though deferential tone adopted by Lemuel, had interested the women intensely in the good-looking youth; and when to this was added the whiff of impiety, the fascination was complete, and the measure of their curiosity full to overflowing.

The morning following the party at Richmond, even before he had risen, Lemuel's servant brought him a note.

'Mr and Mrs Bland request the honour of Mr Leverson's company at dinner.'

'First blood, by Jove!' Lemuel exclaimed, starting to his feet as he spoke. 'I thought it would be so, I knew it would be so. What ninepins they all are! Down they shall go one by one. Defy, defeat, deride the women, and they will worship you even as the Olympians bowed down before the throne, or trembled at the nod of Jupiter!'

Daphne Bland had a pretty little house in Mayfair. Situate in one of those streets where pretty little houses abound, it had nothing to distinguish it exteriorly from its neighbours; but within it was coquettish all over. When you entered there was an atmosphere of refined luxury that found expression in a profusion of

Turkish rugs and Persian mats and screens from Japan; and in the subdued lights were to be distinguished well-stuffed sofas and cushions of eider down, and quiet unpretending nooks and quaint corners deftly arranged for two. It was the house of a widow rather than a married couple, and Daphne was in fact enjoying in advance some part of that freedom to which, in the course of nature, she looked forward some day. Not that her husband attempted to exercise over her any unusual or unreasonable restraint, if we may except the ban upon dancing; but she was tired of their quiet life together, their early hours, their silent breakfasts, their wearisome dinners. When her husband was confined to his room with his periodical fit of the gout, Daphne was wont to snap her fingers and make holiday; to her it was a rift in the clouds, a glimpse of a better time to come; and a fast supper-party not uncommonly marked the more acute stage of his disorder.

Miniver Green was a prime favourite on an occasion of this kind. Miniver was a recognised *flâneur* and wit in society. He had been a clergyman at one time; but having found the occupation unsuitable, or, as was whispered by the malicious, having been himself found to be unsuited to the calling, was now a noted man about town. On occasion, however, Miniver could still maintain much of the mien of his former profession when, for example, Mr Bland's state of health permitted of his presence at the dinner-table. But place Miniver Green with a band of congenial revellers, and nine companies out of ten would vote him into the chair.

On the present occasion Bonnie Beauclerc was the only other guest. She was a cousin of Daphne's, and had just come forth from the nursery. Bonnie was a lovely girl, tall and slight and fair as a flower. She had, as yet, been seen but little in society, and already the town was talking and designating her as the belle of the year. Of snowy white and extreme simplicity was her attire, and she needed no further adornment, for on her brow was the garland of youth, and it was fairer than the opal and the diamond.

Miniver Green sat by the hostess, while Lemuel monopolised the attention of the beautiful *débutante.* Mr Bland had the gout.

'It is very inconvenient for the Mowbrays,' Miniver remarked, 'this defeat of the Government, for they seem to me to exist upon their official position. They remind me of the works of some of our modern sculptors, whose statues never seem capable of standing without the aid of a prop provided for them to lean against.'

'True,' said Daphne; 'and should there be a change in the Government, it would make a considerable difference to the Mowbrays. But, after all, they are wealthy; they will always keep a good house and a French cook, and the world will continue to appreciate such substantial elements of enjoyment, even when no longer flavoured with the seasoning of office.'

'The politician out of place, and with no very immediate or certain prospect of return thereto, is discounted forthwith, if he be not dishonoured,' said Miniver. 'Should he be a duke it does not matter, it is true; but if he be a Commoner, the fall may be fatal to him. Men are but men, my dear Mrs Bland; and women are but women, you know.'

'But Mowbray will be in the next Liberal Cabinet?' inquired Daphne innocently.

'H'm! He might have been included in the last for that matter,' continued Miniver, 'but he wasn't. No; for myself, I think that Mowbray is played out.'

'You don't mean that!'

'The fact is that Mowbray has been an overrated man all his life,' said Miniver; 'and he has contrived to sustain the popular delusion as to his talents by the maintenance of a judicious silence. He is not a deep thinker, he is a political charlatan and a quack philosopher,—a man that will leave literary remains.'

'Well, when one comes to think of it, I grant that it is not easy to see what there is in the man that he should be selected to hold high office,' said Daphne; 'and as for his wife—'

'Charming woman!' Miniver exclaimed, gazing into space as he spoke. 'Dear me! dear me! She has her faults, but still she is very charming, — delightful woman is she not?'

'Well,' said Daphne petulantly, 'you seem to have made up your mind on that point, and I have no desire to question your taste; but you will hardly find many to agree with you. For myself, I think Marcia Mowbray is the most objectionable woman in London.'

' Indeed ! '

' Oh, quite ; she is truly detestable,' said Miss Beauclerc ; 'so rough, so vulgar, you know.'

' One would not tolerate her if it were not for her husband's position, and all that,' said Daphne. ' And then, to be sure, she has a good house.'

' Such a good house ! ' echoed Miss Beauclerc. ' But I should be sorry to be her daughter and have to share it with her, all the same.'

' But may I ask the reason ? ' interrupted Lemuel deferentially.

' Oh, indeed you may,' Miss Beauclerc replied. ' She is the most selfish— '

'The most heartless,' added Daphne.

'The most untruthful,' continued Miss Beauclerc.

'The most intriguing,' said Daphne.

'Quite the most aggravating,' cried Miss Beauclerc, stamping with her pretty little foot.

A loud knocking here interrupted the further enumeration of Mrs Mowbray's weaknesses, and in an instant that lady herself, attired in gala costume, was shown into the sitting-room.

'My dearest!' exclaimed Daphne, casting her arms round Marcia Mowbray's neck.

'My darling!' cried the latter, as she turned to embrace Bonnie Beauclerc, who fell into her arms. 'How fortunate I am to find you both here. I called as I was passing on my way to the Duchess of Shetland's concert.'

'Ah, then, we shall meet again to-night!' Daphne exclaimed with ardour. 'How delightful!'

Lemuel had not been idle during this scene; he had gained a further insight into the ways of society, and the more he studied them the stranger the science appeared to him, and the wider the field for exploration. It is, indeed, a play-ground for the wise, and to the winners in the game the award is, perhaps, worth the effort. This Lemuel understood, and that the man who has society at his feet is already on the road to distinction. And to acquire distinction, see the footsore and the weary travellers as they toil unceasingly along the dusty highways of life; it is pitiable to contemplate their plight, in sunshine and storm alike. But for Lemuel distinction was not to be thus achieved. Let others attain it, if they may, by laborious industry, or the drudgery of an ordinary profession, he would scale the high places by the leaps and bounds of genius. For there was in him a reserve of force such as when other men had exhausted their powers would, he knew, enable him to walk over their prostrate forms and snatch the prize. Hence the marvellous patience and imperturbable temper with which he abided his time. He knew that it would come, and he awaited his turn with a cynical smile that drove less gifted mortals to desperation. Nay, more, he could indulge his fancy for fantastic eccentricity, and even then be more than a match for the common-place and the sober. To men of observation he presented an interesting subject for speculation ; to the methodical and the dull he was an abomination and an offence. Among the former Lemuel had fast friends, even though they might hesitate to believe in his eventual triumph ; but by the latter he was hated and reviled. He repaid their vituperation by brilliant abuse, which made the world laugh, and it came to be understood at length that Lemuel Leverson was better let alone, he was not a man whom it was safe to quarrel with. He was regarded as one of those favourites of fortune to whom success seems to come as a habit ; to whom the worst that happens is a check in the tide of prosperity, and even that seems only to bring out in stronger relief their ultimate victory.

The study of mankind was Lemuel's

daily occupation at this time. To humour them, to flatter, and then to use them for a purpose, were the aims he had constantly in view. And to him they appeared to be legitimate. He did but seize upon the opportunities of life, which other men suffered to pass by unheeded; he made use of the materials that every-day events placed in his hands, and he did so without injuring any man wantonly. The women must be won to his side—that Lemuel regarded as an essential element of success, and he found it by far the easiest part of his task. No good-looking young man that lays himself out to please need have misgiving on that point; and Lemuel had no sooner become known to society than he was taken up by the women, and welcomed with acclamation.

CHAPTER V.

THE tinkling cymbals were in full play, and Marcia Mowbray was receiving her guests with lively condescension at the top of her staircase, when Lemuel bowed to the hostess of his first ball. A continuous stream of the best-dressed people in London was passing into the brilliantly-lighted rooms, and Lemuel quickly found himself in the midst of a multitude, wherein he did not recognise one. An undefinable air of good society pervaded the throng—everybody perceived it, and everybody was pleased.

Those who frequented the best houses habitually felt at their ease, and they who found themselves in good company only now and then felt flattered. A stranger is marked down at once in such an assembly; a new face is scrutinised and criticised, and each woman demands of her neighbour, Who is this? There is a certain lull in the conversation as the un- known draws near, for the common-place, the platitude, even the scandal of the hour has to be exchanged of a sudden for the more interesting topic. The youth is good-looking, perchance; he may be wealthy as well,—at least he may become the fashion, and each and all of these are reasons why he is to be received with civility.

Lemuel was as yet hardly of an age for women to ask of each other whether he were married : that is the real attainment of man's estate. But still, Who is he ? Mrs Mowbray has been catechised a dozen times at the least in the course of the evening.

'Mr Leverson, a friend of the Duchess of Shetland,' is her constant reply.

The answer leaves little to be desired, and Lemuel is presented in rapid succession to rows of ball-giving matrons. But it is whispered that he does not dance. Presently he is observed to take Egidia down to supper, and it is surmised forthwith that he is a millionaire, for Egidia had not been known to patronise thus the impecunious. The rumour spreads with a rapidity that is amazing, and, ere the dawn, but one question remains to be solved, Is his wealth already in possession or only in expectancy ? It is the point upon which society has been unable to make up its mind, and the matrons are contradicting each other, and nobody knows for certain. Crispeyn Caramel, who makes it his business to know everything about persons who are to be met with in society, has it from a sure source that Lemuel's father had died only the year before, and that his capital invested in consols yields a clear forty thousand a-year.

More and more kindly grow the glances of the ball-giving rows of matrons as the rumour circulates, and Lemuel is quite a favourite already.

Egidia had been dancing with Lord Cotswold, but she had danced with him through ten seasons and nothing had come of it. She was tired of Lord Cotswold. They met every night, and he gaped and giggled from the beginning of the ball to the end, supper alone excepted, and then he gobbled. It was with real pleasure that Egidia exchanged his society for Lemuel's in the supperroom, whence, instead of returning to the dance, Egidia wandered with her partner into the conservatory.

For a London house the conservatory was of unusual extent, and it was pleasantly arranged with sofas and easychairs half hidden beneath the tall ferns and giant fuchsias. The lights in shaded lanterns shed a mild glow round the place, less silvern than the moon's ray, and hardly more luminous.

In the centre a trickling fountain cast its threads of crystal into a tiny dell of moss and lichen, whence the stream passed with a gentle murmur into a bason of alabaster, while from a distance came the strain of Weber's soft music, that seemed to breathe love and to inspire passion at every bar. Like the breath of a summer wind it rose and fell, and the time was marked continuously by the beat of the dancers' feet.

To Lemuel, who was keenly alive to the beautiful, and was moved by music as by no other influence, the sensation was entrancing. What if there had been by his side such a one as he had often-times imagined to himself in the sweet summer nights when the moon was at the full? Or such a face as we have

most of us seen for an instant in some
crowded street, it may have been, never
to be found again in all our life after;
a face in which all heaven seemed open,
wherein all that is lovable on earth was
contained ? Egidia could not boast any
of these charms, but the illusion of the
hour was dispelled altogether when her
pointed questions indicated unmistakably
a desire to ascertain the amount of
Lemuel's worldly possessions, both immediate and prospective.

If he had suffered dreamy sentiment to
overshadow him for a moment under the
influences surrounding him, he was quickly
recalled to himself by Egidia's sharp accents that fell upon his ear with the rattle
of the cash-box. Egidia had been struck
by the young man's beauty, and even

fancied she had experienced the first beginnings of love, but she had served no vain apprenticeship; Marcia Mowbray's lessons had not been lost upon her daughter; Egidia had ever proved a ready pupil. It was not the man that had to be sought, it was his gold; it was not the heart that had to be searched, it was the pocket. With the practised skill of an adept Egidia applied the searching probe, and not even the latent fear which cowed her in the presence of this man made her hesitate when the quest was for gold. The diagnosis was unsatisfactory, and from that hour Lemuel was relegated to the second category of the young men of the ballroom, that of the acceptable, but not marriageable youths who amuse and enliven, are agreeable to

sup with, and eligible to fill up the intervals of the dinner-table which the eldest
sons have vacated.

But Egidia's newly-acquired information
had not as yet become common property,
and the matrons still smiled encouragingly,
and their eyes twinkled covetously when
Lemuel reappeared in their midst. Their
eyes grew brighter, indeed ; but it is not
by woman's eyes that a man should be
guided. Observe the lines that play round
her mouth : there is the truth made manifest ; there is the expressive feature. She
cannot conceal them if she would : they
are the ever-faithful witnesses even of the
faithless. But as the season advances the
enthusiasm of the matrons grows cool, for
Crispeyn Caramel has been better advised;
Lemuel has been weighed in the scales

and found wanting, and his place in society is stereotyped from that hour.

To Lemuel the bye-play of the matrons and the subtlety of the maidens had been as a whole library of instructive knowledge, for beneath that impassive mien, that silent gaze into space, there glowed a keen and watchful spirit. He had observed their action from the beginning. He had seen their struggles for information, and enjoyed their chagrin when they came to know the whole truth, and to discover that they had overreached themselves and been cajoled.

While men and women played and plotted Lemuel laboured and reasoned, laughed and grew serious, but no feature moved. With the majority of women Lemuel was too reticent to be quite a

favourite; but to the few for whom the
veil was drawn aside in part the depth
and the variety of his humour had a
resistless charm.   To none was his whole
nature revealed; from the most intimate
there was still a reserved side of his inner
self that kept alive an interest and a curiosity which were heightened by the flights of
exuberant fancy, wherewith at unexpected
moments he would startle and astonish.
For Lemuel there were in the regions of
thought immeasurable solitudes, rich with
fantastic growths of the imagination;
peaks that touched heaven, valleys too
profound for human eye to penetrate
their uttermost abysses.   He looked over
the heads of other men, and beheld a
never-ending prospect of which they knew
nothing, whose shadows alternated with

the meridian sun, a region filled with delight, and the perpetual joys of an abounding fancy. Men said he was eccentric ; but eccentricity would seem to be the almost necessary adjunct of genius ; for how can the gifted mind accommodate itself to the level of the dull ? Fly from the beaten tracks of men ; dive into the depths of primeval forests ; abandon the valley and the plain for the skies of the Alps or the Andes, and you are classed with the eccentric of mankind. You alarm your friends ; they are concerned for your sanity, and they can with difficulty sustain the even tenor of their way in your company. ' What will he not attempt next ? ' cry the staid ones. ' Let us be on our guard ; let us arm ourselves against him,' they say, ' with

the triple brass of sedulous sobriety.'
But genius, unconcerned, advances on
its lofty course, and its head is among
the stars. Aside, ye groundlings! Give
place; for a king of men passeth on his
way!

Before the season had come to an end,
Daphne Bland was a widow. The last
attack of the gout had proved fatal to
her husband, and Daphne sat behind her
pink blinds peering at the visitors that
called to condole with her affliction.

As soon as the obsequies had been
duly celebrated, Lemuel attended to perform the same polite duty, and to his
surprise was told that Mrs Bland would
see him.

Lemuel was shown into a room that
had been partially darkened, and he had

not waited for the space of a minute when a door opened, and Daphne Bland made her appearance.

A tightly-fitting robe of black, over-spread with crape, displayed her neat figure to advantage, and a white tuft of the same material prettily relieved her clustering brown hair.

'It is very kind of you to call,' said Daphne, holding forth her hand; 'indeed, my friends have all been very kind to me. Pray, sit down.'

The widow placed herself upon the sofa, with her back to the light, and beckoned to Lemuel to take his place by her side.

'You may be surprised at my desiring a personal interview at this time,' said Daphne. 'Probably you did not expect to see me ; but a woman feels very much alone in the world at a moment such as this, and she cannot be expected to confine herself altogether to the society of her servants and her solicitor. I have very few relatives, and they are, for the most part, too widely scattered to be available either to assist or to console.'

Here Daphne paused for a moment, and then resumed.

'You cannot imagine what a change it makes in a woman's life to be thus suddenly thrown upon the world, and to find that unwelcome independence that leaves her mistress of herself and of her fortunes. I am quite unnerved at times when I contemplate my position.'

Daphne moved uneasily in her seat as she referred to her isolated state ;

and Lemuel continued to gaze steadily at her, trying to divine the drift of her discourse.

'I have, it is true, an experienced man of business in the person of my solicitor,' continued Daphne ; ' but, then, a lawyer is only a lawyer, you understand; he won't incur the responsibility of giving advice, save only on a point of law. His fee does not cover more than that ; the rest is the office of friendship that has no price ; and with sentiment he declares the law has nothing to do. I am desolate ; I am almost desponding.'

Daphne rested her head on her right hand as she thus gave expression to her feelings, and a deep sigh escaped her.

Lemuel looked on in silence. He was wondering to himself still what was her object in seeking this interview.

'Women are so dependent,' Daphne added; 'men are so helpful, when they care to be so.'

'If,' interrupted Lemuel, lest his silence should be misunderstood, 'there are any means by which I can be of service, pray command me.'

'Oh,' said Daphne, 'you are, I know, the kindest of friends, and would, I am assured, aid me if I needed help. I should not have sought this interview had I not been convinced of that.'

Daphne's voice faltered here, and a little convulsive sob impeded her utterance.

Lemuel was at a loss more than ever to conjecture her meaning; he regarded her with increasing interest. It could not, surely, be that she hinted at marriage?

Why, her husband had not been a week in the grave. The notion was incredible.

'It is a great trial,' Daphne continued. 'My husband has left me everything— everything that he possessed, without condition or reserve, and I fear that I am not equal to the responsibility of it. Indeed, I am overwhelmed.'

'You need the services of an agent whom you can trust,' said Lemuel.

'More than that,' Daphne replied, with a sigh; 'much more. I need one by my side to whom I might confide unreservedly my cares and anxieties. If I thought that you would consent,' continued Daphne, looking nervously on the ground; 'if I thought that you would not refuse—'

Here Daphne's hesitation increased, and to Lemuel it appeared as if, indeed, the day of his destiny had arrived of a sudden. Did she really mean to suggest marriage ? Lemuel had only come to deposit a card, to make a civil inquiry; he was not prepared to find himself brought face to face with the grand question of life, to bound, as it were, into the middle stage of existence, without a moment's warning. But Daphne was wealthy, and Lemuel well understood that riches are the steps whereby men ascend most readily the ladder of fame. It was not for him to refuse. The opportunity was a brilliant one, and he was not going to suffer any of the chances of life to pass him by. He would be true to his destiny. To many a man there comes a moment in life, a turn in the tide of existence, when all depends upon a yes or a no. To Lemuel it seemed as if such an hour had struck for him. At a glance he took in the whole situation; his mind was made up; and, with a composure that might almost have been mistaken for indifference, he awaited the sequel of Daphne's speech.

'You will not be angry with me,' she continued, playing with a fold of the crape on her gown as she spoke; 'I trust our acquaintance is sufficiently intimate to excuse what I am about to say?'

'I am sure that nothing you can say, dear Mrs Bland, would make me angry,' replied Lemuel, who was now close beside her on the sofa.

'I have thought over the many who have flattered, perhaps admired me,' said Daphne, blushing slightly. 'I have seen through their interested motives; but in you I have noticed an independence, a high-minded self-respect—'

'It is even as I conjectured,' thought Lemuel. 'It is destiny—it is fate.'

'Yes, do not hesitate to answer me truly,' Daphne continued, looking with an air of entreaty at Lemuel, who was now preparing to throw himself, after the orthodox fashion, at her feet,—'if I ask you to be— my private secretary.'

CHAPTER VI.

EMUEL was not a favourite with Crispeyn Caramel. To him, indeed, Lemuel was no longer the same man, since it had transpired that he was heir to only a modest inheritance. Crispeyn understood wealth, and he understood high connection, but outside and beyond these two, he desired no friends.

With Crispeyn, who had the ear of society, it rested to a great extent to make or to mar the career of a young man in the world of fashion. And society trusted

Crispeyn implicitly—it detected in him the instinct of safe mediocrity that never rises above a convenient level, and it recognised that he was not likely to introduce within its borders any incongruous element. That he should have committed the mistake of presenting Lemuel to his friends as a millionaire was, Crispeyn conceived, damaging to his reputation, and he resented the self-imposed deception accordingly.

Crispeyn was himself well connected; but, being a younger son and very poor, was deferential in the presence of the possessors of riches. He bowed to the ground before the bankers, the blue blood of Lombard Street and Cornhill, and at their feet he poured invitations for ball and concert with the fecundity of a cornucopia. In the city, Crispeyn was regarded as a messenger from the gods, whilst by the ball-giving mothers of the West End he was welcomed as tout for the rich traders of the East.

Intellectually, Crispeyn was poorly endowed, but his social qualifications were of a higher order ; indeed, they were at once singular and special. All his spare time was taken up in the acquisition and transmission of social knowledge, and the promotion and arrangement of social gatherings. No rumour of the streets escaped his ears ; no scandal afflicted society that was not retailed by his lips. With the elderly women, who were no longer able to scavenge the town for themselves, Crispeyn was a mighty favourite—into their ears he poured the loose gossip of the day, as they reclined in their easy-chairs, or chuckled on their well-padded couches, and

Crispeyn's information was the best of its kind. It was delivered in the voice of an infant, indeed, but it was in its way both racy and refined. In society, he had succeeded in creating for himself a position which was unique ; by the men, it is true, he was contemned for his effeminacy, but the women were his friends, and to the world at large he was known as the Dowager's Delight.

For such as he, the presence of genius has a secret terror in it ; and for them it only remains to shuffle out of sight, or to lapse into silence. There is an end of their peace ; they wither away and subside, and gather into corners, and of their light and airy conversation not even a whisper survives. There is a disturbing element present, and it must be removed ;

genius must be banished at any cost from the region of finical frivolity, for

'Blockheads with reason wicked wits abhor;'

and the Crispeyns must live and pursue their calling.

Crispeyn Caramel felt that he was overmatched and outweighted in Lemuel's presence. Lemuel was silent and reserved, but it was the reticence of a power that gathered, and was all the more irresistible when the time came to strike. It was a positive pain to Crispeyn to find himself in the same company with Lemuel at last, and it was in vain that he essayed to assume an attitude of indifference. He determined to relieve himself at a blow of the presence of a man whom he had learnt to regard as at once a difficulty and a danger.

Warily Crispeyn went to work, for it needed circumspection, and a premature discovery might have been attended by consequences fatal to himself; he might have been scorched by a flash such as of old proceeded from Olympus. But Crispeyn knew his trade,—therein he was no mean artist,—and soon the whisper ran from house to house that Lemuel was an adventurer. Society shies at the word, and coils itself up, as it were, at the bare mention of it; society shrinks and shudders like the sensitive plant at the touch of the adventurer. The rumour runs, and, as a rule, you cannot trace whence it comes; but its victim dies assuredly, unless he can crush it with his heel. Soon the festive banquets are no more, and the ballrooms close, and the three-cornered notes cease to fall like a shower on his writing-table. A plague has stricken him, and he is become an unholy thing, with which it is not seemly for the well-behaved to come into contact.

The chill in the social atmosphere soon made itself felt, and to Lemuel's quick perception its effects were immediately apparent. He was not for a moment in doubt as to its author; Lemuel could have laid his hand upon him from the first, and from that hour kept him steadily in view. Crispeyn tittled and tattled and whispered malice, and Lemuel waited for him with saturnine serenity.

And now, to crown his offences, Lemuel had entered into intimate relations with Daphne Bland. Crispeyn had himself cast eyes upon the widow from the first, but he had been forestalled and outrun, it seemed, by this adventurer.   Daphne was young, she was well-bornand good-looking, and now wealthy as well.   To Crispeyn it appeared that the position taken up by Lemuel as the youthful widow's confidant and secretary was fraught with a twofold danger—the one to society, the other to himself.   As chief director and arbiter of social life at its centre, Crispeyn regarded it as a part of his duty to discountenance and disallow matrimonial alliances from which society would be liable to receive a shake and a shock.   It was a reflection upon himself, he thought, that a young woman situated as Daphne was should marry out of the social set ; that she should run imminent risk of falling into the hands of a Hebrew adventurer, caused him a perceptible shudder. But in this case Crispeyn had, as we have said, a deeper motive still that urged him to action. He wanted the widow for himself, and success was, he felt, out of the question so long as Lemuel sat by her side. He had even a misgiving as to whether Lemuel did not owe him a grudge—had not found him out, in fact—and his conscience suggested as much; but the prize was worth the winning at all hazards, and Crispeyn had been too successful in life to be disheartened where only an adventurer stood in his way.

Lemuel had quickly made himself master of the details of Daphne's affairs. The property was considerable, both in real and personal possessions, and Daphne welcomed gratefully the relief to her mind which she had experienced from Lemuel's

careful and energetic management. But
her peace was not to be undisturbed.
Rumours had commenced to circulate reflecting on Daphne's intimacy with Lemuel.
The whispered scandal had not as yet indeed reached her ears, and by Lemuel it
was encountered with scornful defiance.
Again the idle report seemed to have died
away for lack of substance, when one day,
on entering Daphne's sitting-room, Lemuel
perceived that she had been weeping. An
open letter lay upon the table before her,
and, on perceiving Lemuel's presence,
Daphne buried her face in her hands and
sobbed aloud.

Lemuel was at a loss to conjecture what
might be the cause of this sudden outburst
of grief; he attributed it to some reminis-
cence of her past life which had, perchance,

been recalled to memory, and he attempted to withdraw; but Daphne, looking up with streaming eyes, made a sign to him to approach. She pointed to the letter that lay before her, and again her tears flowed freely.

"Situated as you are," the letter ran, "you can hardly be too circumspect. Your reputation is dear to your friends, but is now in great peril. The world is talking uncharitably; do not give colour to calumny, but remove the excuse for it without delay. You cannot mistake its origin."

Lemuel read the letter a second time, and with deliberation; a shadow passed over his countenance, his eyes gleamed with a little more light perhaps, and his lips were more firmly compressed than before, but no other sign was there that the contents of the letter had affected him. As was his habit, however, his resolution was taken without a moment's hesitation.

' My dear Mrs Bland, I think you should feel that you are indebted in some measure to this writer,' said Lemuel calmly, ' for he has brought to your knowledge a circumstance of which it was necessary that you should be made aware sooner or later. Reports have been circulated to your detriment, founded upon the relations in which we stand to each other. You may be surprised that such should be the case, but now that they display a certain persistency, it is better that I should withdraw from the position which I hold in connection with your affairs. You must risk nothing on my account.'

In an instant Daphne had risen to her feet.

'I will never yield to this infamous chatter,' she cried, brushing away the tears from her beautiful eyes; 'I will hurl the slander back upon those who invented it. No; let them come and accuse me to my face, if they dare. I will never give way before backhanded calumny!'

Seizing the letter as she spoke, Daphne tore it to fragments and cast them to the winds.

'I honour the spirit which dictates such sentiments,' said Lemuel; 'it is worthy of you; but he that is capable of slandering a woman anonymously, is not more likely to come forth at her bidding and show himself in the light of day, than to meet her defender at the sword's point. I owe you a duty; allow me to perform it: I am no longer your private secretary.'

Daphne understood Lemuel's' spirit of determination too well to attempt to resist, or to induce him to recede from the decision at which he had arrived deliberately. She would have surrendered gladly the half of her possessions to have laid her hand on the anonymous scribbler, and dragged him into the light. As it was, she had but to yield, however unwillingly, to circumstances that were too strong for her, and to do so with such grace as she might. But with Lemuel the case was otherwise. From the first he was satisfied in his own mind as to the authorship of the letter, and proof only was needed to enable him to inflict condign punishment. To obtain this might, indeed, be a task of some difficulty, but that the proof would be forthcoming all in good time, Lemuel did not permit himself for a moment to doubt.

CHAPTER VII.

LORD BEAUPORT was the eldest son of the Earl of Corfe. He was a young man of ability, and capable of acquiring distinction in any line wherein he chose to exert his talents. He had gone through the usual course at Eton and at Oxford, and had displayed, after a fitful and capricious fashion, his superiority to his fellows. But Lord Beauport was, above all things, an indolent man. Fond of pleasure, the exertion of earnest application and honest work was distasteful

to him. He was extremely good-looking
and perfectly good-tempered, a favourite
with men and women alike. As Member
of Parliament for the little county town
of Bedborough, he had sat in the House
of Commons for some years, taking part
rarely, however, in the business of the
House. His career in Parliament was,
in fact, a continuation of his career at
the university—without any settled purpose. He took up questions fitfully, and
treated them fancifully ; he was seldom
at pains to investigate them thoroughly.
The House of Commons recognises at
a glance a *flâneur* of this kind; he is
assessed at his true value, and his words
carry no weight. It laughs at his pleas-
antries, for it is a singularly good-
humoured assembly, and it appreciates

his points, but it is impervious to his appeals, and is unmoved by his philippics.

It was thus that Lord Beauport failed to make any considerable figure in Parliament. He was himself conscious of the effect of his levity, and resented it at times; for there were moments when he would have his words taken seriously. But he found the House unrelenting.

The stage in life had now arrived, however, when, in the opinion of his family and of his friends, it was incumbent upon Lord Beauport to marry; and, on the whole, he was disposed to agree with them. His life hitherto had been wayward and unsatisfactory, and he welcomed the change which marriage involved. It is an occasion upon which a man may alter his habit of life if he will, and it is, as a rule, a man's last chance of reform. The man of evil habits who marries and lives as before is usually past redemption ; but the world is disposed to take him at his word should he be serious. If he has been a drunkard, men will not laugh though he talk of becoming sober ; and should he have been a spendthrift, no man sneers when it is said that he is now careful.

Lord Beauport had been extravagant, it is true, but not excessively so, and he was heir to a great estate. By society he had ever been welcomed as the first of blessings, and the matrons and the maidens were radiant in his company ; but their blandishments had been un-attended by success — Lord Beauport

would not marry until a fitting time had
arrived, and then he would choose for
himself. And he would choose deliberately — he would not be driven; and
herein it was that the matrons and the
maidens had made a mistake. They
tried to take him by escalade when
stratagem had failed; and the ladders
were produced, and the forlorn hope was
told off for a desperate venture. It was
at this time when, alarmed at the violence
of the assault, that Lord Beauport renewed his acquaintance with Daphne
Bland.

Fresh from the seclusion of widowhood, she encountered old friends timor-
ously at first. Widowhood is, in fact,
for the young, a reintroduction to society with greater freedom than the first,

and with greater experience. It com-
bines shyness with confidence, it dispenses
with protection, and yet seems to appeal
for it. And herein is the secret of the
widow's success. The girl trusts to her
good looks, her sweet and tender ways,
to gain man's heart; but the widow pleads
her widowhood, she appeals to man's
natural function as woman's protector,
and the widow carries the day.

Daphne was wealthy now, and she
was ambitious. From behind her pink
blinds she had watched the pretenders
to her hand as they trooped to her
threshhold, and she laughed when she
saw them. But with Lord Beauport she
was serious. He was precisely the sort
of man that most readily engages a
woman's interest—nay, it may be, sets

her heart in a flame—a handsome scape-
grace. She longs to try what she can
make of him—to reform him, as she
says—and to have the credit as well as
the pleasure of the task. Lord Beauport's
faults were grave, Daphne knew, but
there was a foundation of easy-going
good nature and thriftless generosity to
work upon. It was wantonness rather
than vice that had to be overcome;
and where a man's heart yet beats with
undiminished warmth, no woman need
despair. It is her opportunity, and she
knows that, if she will it, she can, sooner
or later, make him what she would.

Daphne had made up her mind now,
and a little more than a year had elapsed
from the date of her husband's death,
when she made the final move in

the game of life, and the marriage was formally announced. In the face of the matrons and the maidens, Daphne bore away Lord Beauport in triumph, and society welcomed the event with a shout. For the alliance was suitable and *en règle* according to its canons, and soon the congratulations commenced to pour in even more thickly than the previous condolences.

And now Daphne is above and beyond the world's reproaches once more ; she has succeeded in life and the world is full of her praises, and the Crispeyns are cowed and chased away, or fawn for her friendship. But Daphne is not deceived. She understands the world's worship and what it is worth, and she smiles blandly and nods benignantly to the worshippers one by one.

Soon after Lord Beauport's marriage there was a change in the Government, and, for party reasons, it was considered necessary to include Lord Corfe's son in the new Administration. Lord Beauport was decidedly clever, and he could be eloquent when he cared to undergo the necessary exertion; but he was indolent past belief, and his appointment as Under Secretary of State was regarded in ministerial circles as but a sop to Cerberus. The susceptibilities of the family had to be considered; it was intended to be a recognition of the unsparing use which Lord Corfe had made of his inherited influence in favour of the Government candidates at the elections; a recompense which the steady loyalty of his house to the party had amply merited. But nobody expected that Lord Beaupore would be seen the less at Epsom or at Newmarket by reason of his engagements at Whitehall.

As Under Secretary, Lord Beauport's duties were neither onerous nor responsible, for the head of the department was in the Cabinet, and a man of energy and talent. The Under Secretaryship was such an appointment as an earnest aspirant to statesmanship might have coveted, for here was to be acquired, under an able master, the art and mystery of Government. And the trick of it has to be learnt, as in the case of other arts, for neither do men become statesmen *per saltum;* success remains with the industrious. Detail has to be studied at and worked up laboriously, until the broad conclusions acquire shape and symmetrical form that are to constitute the basis of action. But an idle man follows his fancy, and arrives at conclusions without hearing the evidence ; hence he blunders and falls into disrepute. If he be eloquent, he may stave off the evil day, and if he be clever, he will always have a following, but his career will end in failure nevertheless.

To James Mowbray, who had been his immediate predecessor in office, Lord Beauport had recourse for some preliminary guidance.

' The duties are easy enough,' Mowbray replied, ' but you must not attempt to perform them yourself — that is for the department, recollect. It is essential, moreover, that you should have Roundelay on your side.'

' Roundelay ! and pray, who is Roundelay ? ' inquired his lordship.

' Roundelay is the veteran chief clerk, ' said Mowbray, ' and a veritable rhadamanthus with his subordinates, but silver-tongued as a Siren to those in authority over him. The fact is,' continued Mowbray, who had never been on good terms with his subordinates, ' you will find that the office is composed of snobs and fools for the most part, and Roundelay reigns as king of his company.'

' You mean that he is the greatest snob and fool of the number ? '

' Precisely. But Roundelay has some conspicuous qualities. Should the department oppose your views, Roundelay will be found ready to betray his colleagues at the shortest notice, to pander or to peach at pleasure. Therein lies his value.'

'But why should we tolerate such a creature?' exclaimed Lord Beauport with the innocence of an official neophyte; 'why soil our fingers by the contact?'

'It is statecraft, my dear friend, statecraft that demands the sacrifice at our hands. "*Divide et impera*," you know; it is an old maxim, and you will discover ere long that it is a wise one. Were the permanent officials united, the political changelings sent to preside over them would be worsted at every turn. Remember to maintain your balance of forces, and for that end make Roundelay your own. 'Tis easily done. He was mine for the promise of a knighthood, which he has not obtained. Had we remained in office, I should have had to pay the debt; as it is, I am absolved, and pass the obligation on to you. Dangle it before his eyes till they are dazzled, but keep the toy well out of reach until you yourself have no further use for it.'

Lord Beauport had no sooner entered on his office than it devolved upon him to select a private secretary. This is not a simple piece of patronage—a mere appanage of office to be conferred upon the first favourite — as some suppose; to a man of Lord Beauport's habit, the selection of a secretary becomes a matter of paramount importance. His credit, no less than his convenience, is concerned, and to him it may make the difference between success or failure in office. It was without hesitation that, acting on Daphne's advice, Lord Beauport offered the place to Lemuel Leverson.

To Daphne this arrangement was peculiarly grateful, for it presented the opportunity of making amends to the man who had suffered in reputation for her sake. And for Lemuel himself, the position had peculiar attractions.   Henceforth he was not to be a spectator only, he became a participator, as it were—an active agent in the drama of government; he passed, so to speak, behind the scenes, from that hour, as one of the *dramatis personæ.*

By Lemuel, indeed, the value of his new position was thoroughly appreciated ; it was his opportunity, and he understood how to turn it to account. Lord Beauport, on the other hand, treated his promotion with his accustomed levity.   To him the whole system of government was but a play — a comedy all through — and in this view, the piece that failed to amuse was least likely to hold the boards. He laughed when men spoke seriously of statecraft; to him the rulers were but comedians ever busy at their calling.

The ropes are pulled lustily, and the scenes creak on their hinges, as they are shifted this way and that; and the co-medians watch and wait and scan the faces of the crowd whom they delude and dazzle, and listen eagerly to catch the applause. The lights are turned on, and the blue flame and the red captivate the eye with their magic splendours. And lo! the men cheer and the women giggle, and there is jubilation in every face. Presently a mock Timon is provided to temper their levity with grave utterance, and then a clown is sent on, and then a mime; and when the house is in a roar, the comedians laugh to each other behind the scenes, and wink with the eye, and the cheek is puffed out, and the tongue is protruded, and anon the finger is applied to the tip of the nose.—To Lord Beauport the comedians were ever busy at their calling.

He had never regarded the statesman's craft in any more serious light than this, but it interested him deeply nevertheless, for, to trifle with the destinies of millions —to play with the fortunes of a people— he regarded as a game for gods. Indeed, life itself was but a joke in his eyes; for him it had no serious side. It was a round of pleasure, or it was nothing; and, being brief, every hour had to be enjoyed. With its sorrows he had nothing to do; he closed his eyes, turned away and refused to take his share of the human burden. Let those bear it on whom it is laid; he would be no volunteer. He laughed at virtue and at vice alike, for to him this world was a playground, and he did not believe in the existence of any other. Religion he treated with reckless ribaldry, and his blasphemy was infectious, for it was witty. But Lord Beauport's unbelief was not the product of reason or of science: it was wanton and it was wilful. In pleasure alone had he entire faith, and he scoffed at the rest. Sensuality was the soul of his existence, and there must be no hereafter to trouble or to terrify.

The incredulity of Lemuel Leverson was not less thorough than that of his master, but, being founded on an intellectual basis, it regarded with disdain the unscientific conclusions of debased morality.

'Had I been simply vicious,' Lemuel reasoned, 'I should have been a bad man, but a firm believer; for a thoughtless scamp to take upon himself to set aside the convictions of all ages is proof of imbecility. It is not strength of mind that enables such a one to throw off old beliefs, but enervation of its powers; and it is the consciousness of his weakness that prompts him to prop it up by startling speculations. The infidelity of a corrupt man is in the estimation of the wise only part of his corruption. He becomes a warning to others, not an example: he can never fulfil the office of an apostle.'

To Lemuel his new position presented
a ready opportunity of advancement, on
which he seized with avidity. He had
quickly in his hands all the threads of
knowledge, and these he doled out in such
measure and at such times as he deemed
the most expedient. To Lord Beauport,
Lemuel made himself indispensable : so to
do is a canon in the liturgy of every private
secretary. The minister must know what
is necessary for the occasion, but where-
fore should he be further instructed ?
Beyond this the less information he possesses the better. And the reasoning that
leads the subordinate to this conclusion is
sound past dispute.

'If he should come to know as much as I
do, then what further use would he have for
me ? To be thus lavish of the informa-

tion that I have acquired by diligence and observation is to act the part of a spend-thrift, and I should deserve to want.'

And Lemuel was of all men the least likely to commit so obvious a blunder. Was a council to be held, Lemuel provided the arguments; was a speech to be delivered, he supplied the text and improvised the reasoning, and in due course it would reach Lord Beauport at Newmarket through the medium of the penny post.

'By Jove! that speech of Beauport's has saved the Ministry,' exclaimed the Right Hon. James Mowbray, as, arm-in-arm with the Whip, he passed out of Westminster Hall.

It was four o'clock in the morning, and the debate had just resulted in the victory of the Government by a somewhat narrow majority.

'The most surprising thing that I recollect to have occurred in my time,' responded the Whip. 'I hardly knew whether to trust my senses; and, as he proceeded, I positively raised my glass more than once to make sure that I was not mistaken in the man.'

'It was a masterpiece of reasoning,' Mowbray replied; 'and the intimate knowledge of the subject displayed was not less admirable than the logic.'

'Beauport has developed beyond all expectation,' said the Whip; 'and at this rate he will be in the Cabinet some day. His speech to-night is thought to have made a difference in our favour of five and-twenty votes at the least.'

'I suppose it is the effect of marriage,' said Mowbray; 'if so, it does infinite credit to her ladyship.'

'Lady Beauport is not deficient in cleverness, but I can't help thinking that young Leverson has had something to do with it,' added the Whip. 'I have never succeeded in making the young man out quite—he is so reticent.'

'Yes, he seems to me to overact his part somewhat in that respect,' said Mowbray. 'An over silent man is suspected, and in a private secretary there is no more serious fault. He should inspire confidence, not distrust: he should talk much and say little, if he knows his part. As for Leverson we know that he is not a fool, but we have no assurance that he may not be a knave. To have as your secretary a man that outwits you is a mistake, to say the least of it.'

'I know of none greater,' said the Whip, 'except, perhaps, that he should outwit your wife as well.'

Towards the close of the season Lady Beauport opened her house to receive the world of politics and of fashion in a series of brilliant gatherings. Day by day the town was becoming more empty, and the warm summer nights resounded no longer with the laughter of revellers in St James's, or with melody in Mayfair. The politicians, indeed, were still at their posts, and by them Lady Beauport's entertainments were welcomed as among the most agreeable of the year.

These political assemblies present the strangest contrasts. Here are to be found the wise and the foolish, the learned and the empty-headed, the cultivated and the uncouth, the born favourites of fortune and the self-made, and they who have contended with outrageous fortune all their days and have triumphed at last. To some it is the proudest distinction of their lives to find themselves guests for an hour of those gilded saloons, it is the crowning honour and even a high reward; to others it is a step in the ladder that is to lead to still greater things; to most it is a transformation scene, of which, when the curtain falls, there is no distinct recollection, save of tapers and tinsel and a clamour that is as light as the chaff of a summer's thrashing floor. It is the occasion wherein woman's tact enters in and plays its part in the political drama, the felicitous complement of the policy of Cabinets. And happy is the minister by whose side is found one that understands her audience, who can address an ambassador or an alderman with equal facility and can charm both. He is a double-handed man that may afford his rival odds.

It was close upon midnight, and Lemuel was engaged in escorting the Duchess of Shetland to her coach when a brougham drove away, in which Crispeyn Caramel had just taken his seat. The linkman had followed it, entreating some remuneration, which Crispeyn refused with an oath.

'Curse him!' the man replied between his teeth; 'when he engaged me to act the sneak, and to the woman of this house, too, he was ready enough with his promises; curse him!'

Lemuel had caught the man's words as he turned away, and to Lemuel's ears they had a special meaning. Calling the man hastily, he bestowed a liberal reward for a trifling service; but from that hour Lemuel felt that he was on the track that he had sought with such eagerness, and he ran along it now with the true scent of the sleuthhound. There was no break; there was not even hesitation for an instant; there was only the self-command that forbade him to give tongue as the scent grew hot, and he closed upon his quarry.

For a trifle and a kind word poor Jack had been converted into a friend

and ally, and from him it was that
Lemuel learnt the story of the anonymous letter.

As a lad Jack had been in the service
of Crispeyn Caramel's father. He had
received a fair education, and, had it not
been for the society of evil companions,
might have lived all his days in the
household of his patron. As it was, he
had come to make a precarious livelihood
in the streets, and at the doorways of
the wealthy ; and when Crispeyn sought
for an agent of his malice he bethought
himself of this dependent of his family.

In Jack's possession was found the
original of the letter addressed to Mrs
Bland, and it was in the handwriting of
Crispeyn Caramel. With the manuscript
before him, and with as much composure

as if he were inviting him to dine, Lemuel
sent Crispeyn a challenge on the following day.   To Crispeyn, however, it was
despatched in vain.   He denied the ac-
cusation at first, and then declined the
combat.

It was even as Lemuel had predicted;
but Crispeyn gained little by his coward-
ice. Lemuel crushed him to the earth
in a scathing satire, that set the town in
a roar.   Crispeyn clamoured for life, and
Lemuel was content to take him up
with two fingers and deposit him on the
dung-heap.

CHAPTER VIII.

AFTER the Parliamentary session Lord and Lady Beauport proceeded to Weobly, an ancient seat of the family in the Midlands. It was a grand old house of the Tudor age, and the hand of the restorer had never touched its antique gables, or its quaint lattices, or its stately terraces. The mansion remained, stone for stone, as Lord Beauport's ancestor had erected it in the reign of the Virgin Queen, and in its trim gardens were yet to be found the rosary and the maze, in which Elizabeth may have dallied with a Leicester or an

Essex. The terraces were fragrant still with the old-fashioned flowers, such as Bacon loved to see in his garden :—

' The wild thyme, the pinks, the germander that gives a good flower to the eye, the periwinkle, the cowslip, the daisy, the rose, the lilium convallium, the sweet-william red, the bear's-foot, and the like, being withal sweet and sightly.'

It was a garden after his own heart, a never-ending delight to a refined and cultivated mind; and they who have known the joy of it can share the enthusiasm with which the philosopher begins his essay, by reminding us that it was the Almighty Himself that first planted a garden.

The fair summer days were in the meridian of their course, and the sun poured out a flood of life and joy upon field and forest. The ancient woods that crowned the hills or clothed the valleys of Weobly were tossed no longer by the wild west winds, until their weird arms creaked and moaned again in the blast ; now they stood motionless all the day long, gazing into the broad face of Heaven, patient alike of its smiles and its frowns. No song breaks in upon their deep solitudes ; no movement stirs their shadowy depths.

> .   .   .   ''Tis as the gen'ral pulse
> Of life stood still and Nature made a pause.'

It is an hour of inspiration for poets and for lovers ; it is a time of promise for the wearied statesman escaped from the whirl of the town, when the soft breath of the woodland clears his brain, and lends something of its own wild freshness to his well-worn thoughts.

It was at this delightful retreat that Lord Beauport invited a party to meet during the recess. The Duchess of Shetland and Lady Muriel Bellecourt were among the guests; so also were the Mowbrays and their daughter Egidia. It was Lemuel's first visit to Weobly, and he was interested scarcely less in the place and its surroundings than in the assembled company.

Each nook and cranny of the antique edifice had for him a delight of its own, and the very indifference of the habitués of the place seemed to bring into stronger relief the romance and the poetry that pervaded it. But Lemuel was never happier than when he escaped into solitude, to the unreserved enjoyment of his own thoughts, and the limitless flights of a brilliant imagination. At such intervals he would lose himself for hours together in the pathless wilderness of woods, his spirit exulting in its freedom from restraint like some wild bird that had been caged; then returning, he would take his part in the idle tales in which women delight, or listen with impenetrable gravity to the contentious discourses of political pedants.

The company was a mixed one, and amongst those who joined the party at Weobly at this time were Miniver Green and Herbert Stanhope — 'Sanctimonious Stanhope' he was called by his friends. Stanhope had sat in Parliament for many years, and, when he spoke, his doleful accents had a sobering influence on the House, even in its least serious moods. He was strong upon religious questions, and it was but rarely that he engaged in a discussion of any kind without running a tilt against the Pope. Once embarked upon his favourite topic, he dealt weighty blows at the mysterious power that seemed to him to pervade earth and air. He waved his arms and stamped with his foot until the earth trembled, and in his eye was reflected the fierce fire that burnt within him. In the house, however, the audience was scanty when Stanhope was on his legs ; the word passed into the lobby, and men retired at leisure to dine or to sleep. There was time for either. It happened rarely that Stanhope resumed his seat under three-quarters of an hour, and, meantime, it was not unusual for some member to move that the House be counted. Stanhope was impervious,

however, to interruptions of this kind, for
his earnestness was superior to his discretion. But he was not a harsh or
even unsympathetic man ; when he had
delivered his testimony he could be even
genial, as men are wont to be who feel
that they have accomplished a duty and
earned a reward.

The question which had of late agitated
Parliament to its depths was the exaction
of the Parliamentary oath as it stood. It
operated to the exclusion of gentlemen of
the Hebrew faith, one of whom, a man of
the highest consideration, had knocked at
the door of the House of Commons for
admission in vain. To Sanctimonious
Stanhope any relaxation, any variation
even of the accustomed formula, was a
profanation as direct as if it had been

part of the law of Sinai. To him it was apparent that the oath was intended to serve, not as a test of good faith, a pledge binding on men's consciences that they would fulfil their trust, but a sure mainstay of the Christian religion. In his eyes, the taking of the oath in a form binding on the conscience of a Hebrew would be an outrage to everybody else.

'But, after all,' argued James Mowbray, 'we do not pretend, in these days at least, to settle points of theology in Parliament. We have decided to leave such questions to the individual conscience. How, then, are we justified in compelling the Jews to profess agreement with us in matters of faith, or else to remain outside the body politic?'

'Because we are a Christian people!' cried Sanctimonius Stanhope with vehemence.

'But in what sense are we a Christian people?' asked Lord Beauport, 'since all forms of religion are equally free amongst us? True, the Christians are a majority, an overwhelming majority, if you will; but what of that? Will you maintain that as a reason why the minority should be oppressed? Why should we be thus illogical?'

'Because we are a Christian people!' again roared Stanhope, with augmented violence.

'It seems to me,' continued Lord Beauport, 'that in Parliament we need men of business rather than theologians, and, to my mind, eminent Hebrews show in this respect to advantage by the side of even eminent Christians.'

' Eminent Hebrews, eminent Christians, sir! Can I trust my ears?' exclaimed Sanctimonious Stanhope, in excitement. ' Why, we shall be told of eminent Jesuits next ; nay, of eminent Popes! Zounds! sir, am I in my senses?'

' 'Pon my life I doubt it,' whispered Miniver Green to his neighbour.

' You seem to forget, sir,' interposed Lemuel, ' that it is from the Hebrews that are derived the most precious of our laws, and the principles, at least, on which all the rest are founded. Surely, then, the Hebrews deserve special consideration in our legislature!'

' Special consideration ? By no means, sir,' exclaimed Stanhope. ' On the contrary, they should, in my opinion, be treated with special severity. The man who admits the premisses of an argument, parades his major and his minor, as I may say, and denies the conclusion, is less to be excused than he who cannot follow the argument at all. You really surprise me, sir.'

' To me it is clear,' said Lord Beauport, 'that the law affecting the oath, or, for that matter, any other law, should not be relaxed to suit the convenience of any one man, however respectable, or the caprice of any one constituency; but when there is a whole class of men affected—such, for example, as the Jews— and constituencies are found willing to elect them, I think that the case for relaxation is made out. As to the Jews, we should be specially patient ; for they are our elder brethren, after all. But I would put the case in even a stronger form. If an unbeliever were to appear at the table and to refuse the oath, I should oppose any alteration in the established form to suit his convenience ; but if a body of unbelievers were sent to Parliament, I should certainly recommend that a form be provided to meet the case.'

'What! Admit a body of unbelievers to Parliament!' cried Stanhope. 'Are you aware, sir, that even the Pope himself would not tolerate such a proceeding, had he the power to prevent it?'

'My dear sir,' said Lord Beauport, 'I have for some time been of opinion that, in point of intelligent and logical liberality, we in England have much to learn from the Pope. Whatever the Pope does is done upon fixed principles, carried to their legitimate consequences : we in England act upon impulse, often blind, generally illogical. I am weary of our eccentricities, and have learnt to regard with respect the immutable action of Rome.'

Sanctimonious Stanhope was already on his feet.

'That I should have lived to hear an English minister speak of Rome with respect,' he exclaimed, in accents of sorrowful anger ; 'that I should have heard a member of the Government refer to the Pope by name without the usual epithets of execration, is to me convincing evidence of the decadence of this nation. From Popery and from wooden shoes,' added Stanhope, with fervent emphasis as the men rose from table, 'deliver us, good Lord!'

Sanctimonious Stanhope recovered his spirits when he joined the women in the drawing-room. He had liberated his soul, and was now in a mood for relaxation. And it was in these conditions that Egidia invited him to accompany her to the terrace, whither most of the company had betaken themselves already. Egidia seemed to have made up her mind to be agreeable to Sanctimonious Stanhope, but it is not easy to imagine that there could have been much that was of common interest between them. To all appearance she might have selected a younger man for a midnight stroll. But Egidia was steeped in

worldliness too profoundly to be sus-
ceptible, even amid the solitudes of
Weobly, to romantic affection. As for
Lemuel, she feared him at times, when
beneath his quiet smile she imagined
that she could detect the cynical sneer
with which he was wont to regard the
world and its ways. But even if for
a time she lost sight of it, she could
not but be sensible of the hidden force
that dwelt within him, concealed, covered
over, and kept under, as it was, perpetually, and it disturbed her peace.
She felt nervous in his company, she
was never sure of him, or that he might
not assert himself in some unforeseen
manifestation of his inscrutable character.

Lemuel was studiously attentive and
markedly polite; had he not been so,

Egidia would, she thought, have been better pleased. He would then have afforded her the luxury of a grievance against him. But his manners left nothing to complain of, and, could she have trusted him entirely, even Egidia thought she might have fallen in love.

For her the last season in London had been a disheartening failure. It was her tenth, and she had done her best, and had effected nothing. And at the close of a tenth season a girl's symptoms become serious. Her very worldliness is a weariness to her at last; it has lost its freshness, its frivolity has forfeited its flavour. Is there none to deliver her from herself and restore her peace? In such a state of mind a girl will not unfrequently be

rash—she will consent to marry almost
any man that asks her rather than to
recommence in another season the profit-
less campaign.

And such was the humour in which
Egidia found herself when, with Sanctimonious Stanhope, she passed out on
the terrace. His usually austere countenance relaxed sensibly as he accompanied her through the open window,
and he was almost playful when he
placed his chair beside hers beneath the
spreading limes. To him Egidia seemed
to-night to be a singularly agreeable
person; he had not been used to the
delicate flattery with which she assailed
him. Girls had, as a rule, shunned his
society, as they would that of an ogre.
Here at least, it appeared to him, was

one not wholly frivolous. From flattery
Egidia passed to sentiment; and when
the moon is at the full, who shall set
bounds to the power of sentiment? See
the softening lines of Sanctimonious Stanhope's countenance. He has passed
through life unscathed as yet; but now,
forgetful of the Pope, he places his
hand on the back of the chair upon
which Egidia is sitting, and whispers in
her ear.

Muriel had noticed Egidia's action, and
marvelled. To Muriel, with her dove-
like eyes that knew no guile, love was
a fairyland, a dream of passionate
delight, not a business to be transacted
with weights and measures; and when
she beheld Egidia thirsting for this
man's gold, she hated the girl in her

heart. It was a bargain, and nothing more, on Egidia's side; to her it mattered little that—

>   . ·   . ' Love dwells not there,
> The soft regards, the tenderness of life,
> The heart-shed tear, the ineffable delight
> Of sweet humanity.'—*Thomson.*

But how did such considerations affect her? Had she not tried for better things and failed? The men laughed at first, and the women giggled when they perceived that Egidia was in earnest, but reflecting, grew serious; they bethought themselves that she who laughs last often laughs longest and loudest, and they shrewdly suspected that, in a worldly sense, Egidia might have the best of it after all.

From the terrace Lemuel wandered in Muriel's society to the edge of a precipitous descent that led from the garden to a picturesque valley.

'Do you know,' said Muriel, 'that we are now close to the haunted vale?'

'The haunted vale?   Pray, what is that?'

'The valley at our feet, so runs the tale, is haunted by a spectre that has been known to many generations as the White Lady of the Valley.   There is no tradition of her history, but she is described as a beautiful woman with large, sad eyes, that flits across the path, gazes at the wayfarer for an instant as if she sought some lost one, then wrings her hands in an attitude of despair, and vanishes in the nearest thicket.   A former owner of Weobly, who is said to have encountered the White Lady many times, caused a tablet to be erected on the spot commemorative of the tradition.'

'I should like to visit the place,' said Lemuel; 'and in this glorious moonlight, too. You do not object?'

'No,' said Muriel, somewhat timidly; 'not with you to accompany me; but I admit that I should hardly venture alone at this hour. I am not, I think, super-stitious, but where there is said to be something weird and not to be accounted for, I confess to feeling nervous.'

'How I should rejoice to encounter the supernatural,' said Lemuel earnestly. 'Very possibly it would change my whole life,—I should be so much happier could I believe in it. And then, the triumph over reason, — you can't think what a luxury that would be, it is such a tyrant.

Happy women, that are not troubled with it!'

'You are not disposed to pay us compliments to-night,' said Muriel, laughing; 'that is abundantly apparent. You and I are friends, and so it does not matter, but pray recollect that you are now going into a strange lady's society.'

They had reached the entrance to the valley, through the centre of which an open glade stretched away into the distance as far as eye could follow. On either side were giant oaks, whose matted foliage cast a deep shadow, and at intervals the tall pines reared their tufted, heads, whereon the moonbeams rested like snow on the hill-tops. Close at hand was a marble slab, on which were these lines inscribed,—

'Rest, gentle shade, these moonlit glades among,
  Thy fate to us unknown, thy griefs unsung,
  Though violated home thy bosom wrung,
  Or careless husband, or some heartless wrong,
  From faithless friend or ever-wayward son,
  Left but a broken heart and life undone.
  Here where the moonlight makes its silent bed,
  Still rest thee here, pale wand'rer from the dead !
  Sad welcome do we bid thee : kindly hail
  We give thee, gentle Lady of the Vale !'

Lemuel read the lines aloud, and the soft tones of his musical voice added pathos to the verse. He had scarce concluded when, of a sudden, a stag startled from its lair at their feet, bounded across the green sward and through the long fern. Muriel, whose nerves had been shaken already by the associations of the place, uttered a cry of terror, and fell into Lemuel's arms in a swoon.

CHAPTER IX.

BY the following morning Muriel had recovered almost entirely from the effects of the previous night's adventure. The shock had been severe for one of her delicate constitution, but when it was apparent that no evil effects followed, even the duchess smiled, though she had been alarmed at first.

'When young ladies go to seek hobgoblins by the light of the moon they generally succeed in finding them,' the duchess remarked. 'It was fortunate, however, that on this occasion Muriel was so well attended.'

'We stay-at-home people have occasionally the best of it,' Daphne observed, as she and Marcia Mowbray sat together after breakfast. 'There was quite as much sentiment, if less adventure, it appeared to me, on the terrace last night as in the haunted valley. Do you know, it occurred to me that Mr Stanhope himself was not altogether insensible to the influences of the hour when he found himself in Egidia's company?'

'I am sure I wish that it had been so,' Marcia replied, 'for it is quite time that Egidia were married. It is such a trial to have a girl on your hands when, positively, you do not know what to do with her. I have sometimes wished that we had been blessed with a son instead of a daughter. Girls are so helpless and need so much looking after, whereas boys soon learn to take care of themselves. Indeed, the gravity of the situation comes home to me when I see the same girls present themselves season after season to prance and giggle and return as they came. To me the spectacle is full of melancholy, and casts a shade over every ballroom.'

'But is it not better after all that girls should come to town under any circumstances?' asked Daphne. 'In the country they assimilate themselves marvellously to their surroundings and become hopelessly dull. Even their garments partake of the prevailing rusticity. See the London girl draped with the grace of a Grecian statue. She may be plain according to

all the laws of physiognomy, but, notwithstanding, the eye is gratified and satisfied.
Behold your pretty country girl as she
stands by her side in misshapen garments :
with which of the two do the men prefer
to dance ? There is a sweet simplicity,
moreover, about the London style, though
it is coquettish in every fold, that carries
triumph with it. It is a wonderful art
and comes with culture. The ancients
understood the fascination of simplicity,
and when they would have Venus win
the hearts of gods and men she was
clad in the foam of ocean. No; girls
cannot afford to live country lives, of that
I am convinced. They resemble some
delicate fruits that ripen rapidly in the
sunshine — you may almost detect the
golden tints gathering one by one; but

place them in the shade and they become sour and colourless.'

' Then Egidia has been in the shade for some considerable time past,' observed Marcia bitterly. ' I thought for a moment last night that the prospect was brightening a little, but to-day I fear it was only the illusion of the moon. To be sure there are objections sufficiently obvious to an alliance with Stanhope.'

' Few men are more respected than he, remarked Daphne; 'and, although it cannot be denied that he has his peculiarities, and there is a considerable difference between him and Egidia in point of age, still twenty thousand a-year represents a very substantial amount of worldly goods from which to endow a wife. There are advantages, very decided advantages ; and, after all, it is not every girl that can become a duchess, you know.'

'It is precisely what I have preached to Egidia times without number,' said Marcia Mowbray, 'and she seems to have realised the truth of it, though, I confess, somewhat tardily. But see!' Marcia exclaimed, drawing aside the blind as she spoke, 'see, here they come, hand-in-hand too!'

The second thoughts of a night had not, it was evident, lessened, in Sanctimonious Stanhope's mind, the impressions of the previous evening; indeed, as soon as breakfast was over, he had invited Egidia to walk with him in the garden. Now they were observed to pass into the mansion from the terrace, and Daphne made hasty preparations for retreat, with a view to leave the lovers in undisturbed possession of the saloon. She had already risen for this purpose, when, in the reflection of a mirror, she detected Sanctimonious Stanhope in the act of placing his arm round Egidia's waist, and bestowing upon her a tender embrace.

'My dear,' whispered Daphne in some excitement, as she passed with Marcia Mowbray into the corridor, 'that girl is either engaged to Mr Stanhope, or it is time that she should be!'

The relations of Lemuel Leverson and Muriel had not, on his side at least, become sensibly warmer since the incident of the previous evening, and few men who have found themselves under circumstances so interesting in the society of a fascinating girl, have come away with so light a heart. It was a trial such as the strongest have found too strong for them ere now, and have not been ashamed to own it, for there is no steel that ever cased the heart of man through which so subtle an influence will not penetrate. Had Lemuel been as the rest, he too. would have been vanquished—would have fallen at Muriel's feet, and there made known his passion after the customary form.

But it was not by such means that Lemuel would rise to wealth and power; he would be the architect of his own fortunes, and he felt that a day would come when the proudest in the land would feel prouder for the offer of his hand. It was not, indeed, because he was insensible to Muriel's beauty and sweetness, that he was enabled thus to come away unscathed ; on the contrary, he realised more than most men the immeasurable depth and charm of her nature ; but for Lemuel, the hour had not struck, and passion and sentiment were still to be kept well in hand.

Ordinary men might have made demonstrative love ; Lemuel contented himself with writing a sonnet in Muriel's album—

> ' The wand'ring deer when day was done
>   Lay resting by the hallow'd stone,
>   Awaiting still the morning ray
>   To range o'er hill and dale away.
>   When lo ! the lovely queen of night,
>   Is straight eclipséd out of sight,
>   And softer gleams than moonlit skies
>   The lustre of a woman's eyes.
>
> What marvel if the spotted deer
> Wait not the note of chanticleer ?

What marvel if from pointed horn
He shake the dew and greet the morn?
And, bounding straightway from his lair,
Exulting seek the rosy air?
For, not Aurora's self outvies
The lustre of a woman's eyes.

Blame not the deer then, lady fair !
Thy wonderment he did but share,
And sought in vain the glorious sun,
That moon and stars alike outshone.
But least of all may he complain,
Who shared thy momentary pain :
He yet beholds, like Phœbus rise,
The lustre of thy woman's eyes.'

Lemuel's commanding self-control had no counterpart in Muriel, however. Her soft impressionable nature yielded itself up altogether in face of the stern fascination which his presence exercised. Her whole disposition was of the gentle type that goes sufferingly on through life, and makes no sign. An accident it may be, or be it the work of angels or of men, may place

VOL. I. M

her where she so well deserves to be, the proud and happy wife of one that would try to be worthy of her even if he were not altogether so. But it is a work which Muriel will never accomplish for herself; she can but wait upon fortune, and trust to accident. She is not of the heroic mould that compels success. Muriel's was not a nature to grapple with the world, to stand up to it, to take it by the throat, if need be, and prove what a craven it is after all; she would hide herself away, rather, and sorrow in secret, and the world would pass by and know nothing of it. When Muriel read in her album the lines that Lemuel had inscribed there, she laid her head upon the page, and it was stained with her tears.

By Egidia, Muriel's weakness was re-

garded with contemptuous pity. Egidia
was not going to be the handmaid of
Fortune; she would force the fickle god-
dess, not pander to her caprices. As to
destiny, she laughed at it. All Egidia
knew was that the strong succeeded in life,
while the weak went to the wall, and it
was sufficient; therein was an end of the
argument so far as she was concerned.
She had made up her mind to marry Sanctimonious Stanhope; and the advantages
were, from her point of view and under her
circumstances, unquestionable. Seventy-
two summers had passed over his head,
and he had never asked any woman to be
his wife; but Egidia had taken hold of him
and refused to let him go; and this very
day before the guests had assembled at the
dinner-table, the marriage was announced.

Momentous decision, more serious than any of which Sanctimonious Stanhope had a notion! Where had all the sunny days of youth been passed that he should have waited for the winter with its snows thus to begin? Under what delusions did he labour that he should thus mistake—

'Fair days in winter for the spring?'

But Egidia passed radiantly along with this man arm-in-arm; she led him after the manner that the ox was led of old to the sacrifice—crowned with flowers. He was truly her victim, but rejoicing the while in the sense of triumph with which Egidia had inspired him. Brimming over at the prospect of the long-drawn vista of conjugal felicity, he contemplated the flower-strewn smiling future that spread itself before his confiding fancy.

'Fool!' thought Lemuel in his heart; 'at seventy-two to lay out plans and to make preparations for a joyous career! It is about time that these Christians should learn to be not less wise than the much contemned Pagans, their predecessors of two thousand years ago. How musing Horace would have regarded such a spectacle!

> " .   .   O beate Sesti,
> Vitæ summa brevis spem nos vetat inchoare longam.
> Iam te premet nox!"—

But it is as it should be after all,' Lemuel would add. 'If there were not fools in the world wise men would be at a discount, and very familiarity would have brought wit into contempt.

' Then long live our fools ! Their existence relieves the hard lot that fate
imposes upon the poor ; and whether
they will or no, they lend the helping
hand to genius. The wealthy fools are
the appointed prizes, the gold-encumbered
galleons, the deeply-laden argosies, that
fall an easy and profitable prey to the
daring privateer. Wealth is no more
stereotyped in families than length of
days or bodily beauty, and the rich are
the spoil of the skilful as much at this
day as when the highwayman beset the
path. The kingdom of this world is to
the wise, not merely to the wealthy.

' " Whence then cometh wisdom, and
where is the place of the understanding ?
It is hid from the eyes of all living, and
the fowls of the air know it not."

'True, it is the subtle gift of nature, and we cannot predict it of any ; but they that possess it are the born champions of the race, and if they be not worthy of the inheritance, let them perish utterly and be forgotten. The rich fool is not to be lightly condemned, for he too has his purpose ; he is an incitement to the ambition of the wise. But a poor fool is nature's scullion ; let him clean the pots and the pans till he die, and the foolish children of the fool take his place.'

Lord Beauport's generous wine had circulated freely in honour of the coming marriage. All the company were elated, but Sanctimonious Stanhope was in a mood that was exceptionally genial.

'When we meet in London, my dear

young friend,' he exclaimed, turning to Lemuel as he spoke, ' I trust that Mrs Stanhope and I may often have the pleasure of welcoming you beneath our roof. Indeed, I may say that the future Mrs Stanhope purposes to be exceedingly gay. Dear me! I cannot think how I shall get through it all. Dear me! Dear me!'

' Neither can I,' thought Lemuel, ' for the life of me. But I fancy I can see him seated already on a very high stool indeed, with the volume of Job in his hands for light literature.'

CHAPTER X.

THE commencement of the early season is marked by the holding of Cabinet Councils. It is the first decided indication that the time for action is once more at hand.

After the breaking up of Parliament the intercommunication of ministers is fitful and uncertain. The grouse and the partridges are the only verities at this time, and to them the pheasants succeed; but following on the wings of the latter come the anxieties of State and the responsibilities of office, and many a man leaves the covert side with a sigh even for the Cabinet.

'Vive la bagatelle!' said Lemuel to himself when he saw the political puppets putting in an appearance one by one, and taking up the positions assigned to them. 'Vive la bagatelle!'

The gladiators are rubbing up their armour, and the sheen of it gleams through the fogs of December and January. Now have to be devised and moulded into shape the wise shifts of political expediency that, in the ensuing session, are to trim the scales of fortune. But they are sacred and secret until the House meets. The moles are at work, but they cannot avoid throwing up the fresh earth hither and thither in their progress ; and this, do what they will,

attracts the world's notice and points un-
erringly to the goal at which they are
aiming. But mystery has to be maintained, and men take refuge in conjecture. It is the epoch of the political
prophet, be he a Sanctimonious Stanhope
sniffing the air to catch the light winds
of Rome ; who, finding the Government
not wholly orthodox, straightway places
a pan of live coals upon his head, cry-
ing, ' Woe to you ! woe to you ! ' Or be
he some blatant Wilkes denouncing the
government of the few, and predicting
the coming downfall of cabinets and of
kings. But the ministry is sanguine, and
gathers courage as the bustle grows and
the councils multiply.

A popular surprise is deemed good
policy at the commencement of a session,

and during these weeks of preparation the production of the unlooked-for measure is laboriously matured. But the Cabinet was not brilliant; it was sound rather than original in its tendencies, and there was scarce to be found among its members one from whose brain could be struck a solitary spark to relieve the gloom. Fireworks were wholly out of the question. Sombrely they sat, and the weeks sped by on their course, and now in a fortnight the House would meet.

'We are in a bad way,' quoth Nestor, as he shuffled along Downing Street in company with Ulysses when the council was over. 'We are dying of inanition surely and not slowly. This Government has seen its best days, to my mind.'

'We need fresh blood,' Ulysses responded; 'there can be no doubt about it; and it was the idea in the minds of us all to-day as we sat round the board, though no one thought fit to give it expression. There was quite a hungry look in the eyes of some as they regarded their neighbour, such as we read of in the history of famishing crews when it becomes a question who is to die that the rest may live.'

'I think I perceived something of the kind,' replied Nestor; 'and it occurs to me that if some one were to volunteer, the effect might be better than that we should draw lots. It would relieve the Prime Minister of a difficulty and be appreciated by the party. For myself, I confess that I begin to feel the weight of responsibility somewhat heavy for my years. I have had a seat in some half-dozen Cabinets in my time, and I almost think that I can see my way to—'

' A peerage ?' interposed Ulysses.

' You are very good !'

' And—er—a pension ?'

Nestor here arrested his steps, and, seizing the hand of his friend shook it with fervid emotion.

' No, no ; it is not that. The testimony borne by one's countrymen to the efforts, however humble, of a life-time spent in their service is the truest reward,' said Nestor, much moved, as he parted company with Ulysses in St James's Street. ' No!' he added, feelingly, ' give me the hearty goodwill of my countrymen. It is all I ask ; it is my highest ambition.'

'Old fox!' exclaimed Ulysses as he turned into Boodle's; 'he knows we mean to get rid of him whether he will or no. He has, to my certain knowledge, been told as much by the Prime Minister himself. Now he wants to drive a bargain. Hearty goodwill indeed! Excellent joke! But he is right! By Jove! Nestor is right,' added Ulysses, shrugging his shoulders. 'He has not sat in "some half-dozen Cabinets" to no purpose. I have noticed that the State ever honours that man the most who knows how to honour himself. Nestor is in the right, by Jove!'

The fact was, that Lord Beauport's fame had grown rapidly, and men had begun to feel that his presence in the Cabinet would be a source of strength to the Government both in Parliament and in the country. There was a cry among the party for Beauport, which it was no longer safe to ignore. The Prime Minister had decreed it, and ere a week had elapsed, the announcement appeared in the *Gazette*. Nestor had been raised to the peerage by the favour of the Sovereign, and contemporaneously the Prime Minister had the pleasure of communicating to the new noble that a pension of two thousand a year had been conferred upon him for life.

Nestor had been shelved gracefully, and Lord Beauport reigned in his stead. It was a proud moment for his lordship, for even his best friends and well-wishers had not until recently ventured to prophesy such rapid advancement. The frequenter of the racecourse, the idle *flâneur* of society, the wanton trifler of the greenroom — who would have thought that he was destined to form one of that sacred band in whose hands rest the destinies of England? But Lord Beauport took his seat at the board with all the nonchalance of one born to the place, and entered into the discussion of the day with as much coolness as if the subject were the chances of the favourite for the Derby or the Oaks.

The absence of surprise is, indeed, a test of good breeding, and the man who starts and is confused will hardly trace back his pedigree to the Normans. His experiences are of to-day, and the experiences of his ancestors were restricted to those of yesterday; the quality is hereditary. Your ploughman is open-mouthed at the transformation scene, for neither he nor his progenitors had conceived anything better than a raree show.

The presence of Lord Beauport soon made itself felt in the somnolent Cabinet. He had not sat there a week before he recognised the exigencies of the situation, and that his colleagues, sunk into the depths of mediocrity, encumbered with custom and routine, were incapable of rising to the level of the occasion.

'The fact is,' he exclaimed, 'the reins are in your hands no longer; you have dropped from the box, and are hanging on behind, after the fashion of the gutter - boys. You may impede the machine ; you may even succeed in arresting its mad career, but presently, growing languid, you will yourselves fall away, and it will rush headlong to destruction. The revolution has, up to this time, been ahead of you ; you must go forward with a bound and outrun it, if you would save your country and yourselves. Taking it in front and rear, you must smite it with a strong arm.'

The boldness of this advice took the Cabinet aback. It had been used to half-hearted measures. What manner of counsel was this, the like of which had not been heard within those walls for a decade ? Cabinets may not be precipitate, however ; they are not wont to be rash ; and it was determined to postpone a decision. It was Saturday, and happily the Sabbath intervened ; for the Sabbath is a day that is much devoted to sober politics. It is a day upon which political questions harden, are transformed, and pass not infrequently from the abstract to the concrete form. A question already in hand may be elaborated and worked out on the Sabbath, though you may not originate, for such are the ethics of the British Sunday. It is light, not labour, that constitutes the offence.

The value to the British Statesman of the Sabbath is very considerable, more especially when controversies run high ; and, as a rule, the interval of reflection has the effect of bending men's minds towards the proposals of the Government, rather than of the Opposition. The tendency of

the day of rest is to soothe and to settle.
not to foment contentions.

When the Cabinet met again, the
sound judgment which dictated Lord
Beauport's advice had been fully recognised, and it had come, moreover,
just in time to relieve the speech from
the throne from disastrous dulness. As
it was, men rubbed their eyes to be sure
that they were awake, and not dreaming.
The nation was electrified at the boldness
of the new policy, and the party was
enthusiastic. Lord Beauport's reputation
rose with a bound, and already might
be detected the faint glimmer of the
aureola that adorns the brow of the
statesman whom his countryman have
made up their minds to canonise.

The great speech was delivered, and

the popular voice designated Lord Beauport as the popular idol.   He passed
from the House to Westminster Hall,
where an enthusiastic crowd was waiting
to cheer him.   Hats are ra'sed and handkerchiefs are produced, and Lord Beauport bows on this side and on that, as
he advances amid the throng to his carriage.   It is a veritable ovation.   From
Newmarket and the Town Moor he has
advanced already to Olympus, and is
seated with the gods.

Lemuel, who had been present in the
House, followed Lord Beauport at a distance into Westminster Hall, and the
shouts of the populace were still ringing
in his ears, and he had seen the women's
handkerchiefs fluttter in the air.

'Mountebanks!' he exclaimed, 'for

the most part: deceivers or deceived every one. Stay! there is one here that knows better,' Lemuel added, as he placed the manuscript of Lord Beauport's speech in his bosom, and leaped into the hackney coach that was to convey him to the *Times* office.

'In a few hours all England will have read this as the composition and the mind of him who owns it not. 'Tis hard, 'tis bitter to the taste, but it has to be borne, and it won't last.'

As Lemuel emerged from Westminster Hall, he saw Lord Beauport enter his carriage amid the renewed vociferations of the multitude. Therein, awaiting the advent of her husband, was Daphne, and triumph was in her eyes, even though the tears stood there.

'This is the noblest recompense of life's labours after all,' thought Lemuel as he paused for an instant—'to come back from the strife, be it victor or vanquished, to the woman whom you love, and to read in her eyes that she is proud of you. Inestimable rewards, and sweeter than all gifts!

> 'They rob the Hybla bees,
> And leave them honeyless!'

CHAPTER XI.

AT Marcia Mowbray's house Lemuel renewed the acquaintance of his schoolfellow Willie Lambton. He was Marcia's half-brother, son of her father by a second marriage, and very many years her junior. Marcia did not care for her stepmother or for her son; but it was, Marcia conceived, to her advantage that she should be able to refer to a brother who was so much younger than she was; it lessened, she fancied, her own years in the common estimation. Hence it was that Willie

Lambton was invited invariably to her house when Marcia desired to appear at her best.

Years had elapsed since Willie and his schoolfellow had last met; it was then the threshold of life for both, and in the interval each had advanced a stage on the road that cannot be re-traced. Willie Lambton had gone from Harrow to Cambridge, and was now engaged in the practice of the law. He was a delicate and interesting youth of four-and-twenty, with large, pensive, grey eyes, and there was a sadness in them, a joyless expression, so strongly marked as to attract attention at once. The melancholy that tinged his nature softened it also, and led away his thoughts from the enterprise and action of every-day life to a loftier and nobler ideal which he had formed for himself, an arcadia such as poets have imagined, but which practical men have not found to exist on the earth, and thence his aspirations passed on to a paradise beyond the skies such as eye hath not seen. It was his duty, he felt, to exert himself in his profession, however, so as to avoid becoming a burden to his family; but further than this he had no ambition. The events of every-day life he regarded with habitual indifference, looking away and beyond them to a land of dreams. The rough contact of men repelled him; his refinement took alarm, and he shrank instinctively away. He distrusted the world around him, and lived more in the past than in the present—in the literature of another age, the genius of which alone survives when all that is of baser earth has mouldered away.

'I have often recalled the happy days we spent at Harrow,' said Willie Lambton ; 'you and I, when we wandered together, and wondered at the world before us, and speculated as to what was to be our own share in it. And you were sanguine, and I was doubting, and we were both in the right, it seems.'

'The tree can be no other than the seedling,' said Lemuel ; 'it must give forth flower and fruit after its kind ; its nature remains the same in whatsoever soil it may be planted. You and I have passed into the world, and you still doubt and I am sanguine.'

'It is even as you say,' Willie replied; 'it has been so from the first until now. Who knows, however, but that we shall change places at last, and that when my doubts are ended, yours will begin?'

'A man should get rid of his doubts early,' said Lemuel. 'I do not preach precipitation, remember; but doubts become chronic at last; you are their slave, and they can be shaken off no more than the old man in the Eastern tale. The grasp tightens the more violently you struggle, and they will strangle you not improbably in the end. For myself, I have no doubts; my mind is made up. True, I have one only belief, but that one is a sovereign remedy against faltering and feebleness. I believe in myself, and it is the beginning and the end of my faith.'

'Is it possible, then,' continued Willie, 'that you have lost altogether the precious inheritance of your fathers, the hope and expectation of Israel, and that its sublime story has for you no meaning?'

'You are mistaken if you think so,' rejoined Lemuel. 'Of the literature of my people there is no more earnest student than I—none more enthusiastic. Do not misunderstand me. The Hebrew Scriptures are for me the sublimest of poems —more ennobling than that of the blind bard of Chios, and more historically accurate. The joys, the sorrows, the hopes of our race are written in letters of fire, but to me they are a poem still. To you, indeed, they are more, and I am

not surprised : they are so intensely
human that you call them divine.'

Lemuel stood erect as he spoke ; his
eyes flashed for an instant with unaccus-
tomed light, and his whole countenance
beamed with animation.

'How tender and how strong ; how
calm and how enthusiastic !' he continued.
'You may search the literature of all
ages and not find a parallel, open the
page where you will. Read the story
of Joseph and his brethren, and the tears
are already in your eyes. It is the most
pathetic that has ever been written in
which no woman is concerned.'

'Again, we know but little in reality
of the captivity under the Pharaohs.
Yet how that bondage comes home to
us in the wonderful song that commemo-

rates the going out from Egypt—that delirium of joy wherein all nature seemed to take part, and the mountains themselves to leap from their foundations !

' Respond, thou wind-obeying sea,
  What troubleth thy repose ?
Say whence, O Jordan, dost thou flee,
  Thy flood, why backward flows ?

What wondrous awe, what fear affrights
  Thy rest, thou mighty deep ?
And O ye everlasting heights,
  Why skip like lambs of sheep ?

'Twas at the face of Jacob's God
  The troubled waters fled,
And Isra'l's people safely trod
  The ocean's trackless bed.

'Twas at the voice of Jacob's Lord
  Th' exulting hills made known
That Israel had heard His word,—
  The Lord had saved His own ! '

' My dear Lemuel,' said Willie Lambton seriously, ' there is more than poetry here, there is conviction ; and this it is which elevates the sacred writings above the grandest compositions of Greece and Rome. This is no dream, no ingeniously contrived myth. In a sense, indeed, it is more to the credit of the Greeks to have constructed whole systems of religion, with their thousand marvels, out of the imagination; whereas, the Jews did but record the wonderful works that were accomplished in their midst.'

'I am in the habit of doing my countrymen more justice,' said Lemuel, speaking now with deliberation; 'and herein, I apprehend, lies the difference between us. In my view, they were endowed with imaginative powers more fertile than any that you are disposed to give them credit for.'

There was silence for a moment, and

Willie Lambton smiled despite himself at the cynical remark.

'Ah, well!' he exclaimed, placing his arm within that of his friend, as they proceeded homewards, 'I do not despair of you—I will not; I cannot. You have a reverent mind; you are keenly alive to what is beautiful and true; there is nothing, let me say it, that is sordid about you; and when you, too, behold the pillar of light preceding you in the darkness you will follow it, believe me, even to the Promised Land. May it be so! Goodnight.'

'What a fascination there is about him!' thought Willie Lambton, when he was once more alone; 'what a power he possesses for good or for evil—what a responsibility! It is a mysterious influence, and I am afraid of it, I confess. It is the force of character, the master-spirit, that dominates as if it would over-whelm and carry you along with it, whether you will or no, you know not whither. Lemuel has genius, and I have none; but what a price he pays for the perilous possession! I suppose I should be con-tent—nay more, that I should be thankful.'

It was midnight now, and the streets were deserted, save at the corners, where the gin-shops blazed far into the night, and Willie Lambton hastened on his way through the tortuous streets and alleys that led to his home in Lincoln's Inn.

In a quaint row of the old brick houses, of the era of Elizabeth and of James, Willie had his chambers. The

house had no door, or, if there were one,
it had, from long disuse, ceased to be
regarded as a barrier. The ancient stair
was worn by the tread of many generations of lawyers, and the massive balustrade gave signs of yielding, at length,
beneath the weight of years that pressed
upon it. It was a gaunt old house, that
might have had many a tradition of
comedy or of tragedy attached to it
appertaining to the tenants of two cen-
turies and a-half. But tradition there
was none. There seldom or never is
any tradition connected with these old
lawyers' houses. Either hearsay - evidence is not regarded in these precincts
as of value, or the inmates change too
often to preserve continuity of record;
at any rate, these old walls are mute

for the most part,—there is no echo in
them ; even ghosts are not recognised
in the Inns of the Courts. They have
no *locus standi*, and the law takes no
account of them.

Willie Lambton inhabited two rooms
off the third floor landing. The walls
were wainscoted, and the ceilings were
low, and the lattices were yet filled with
the narrow panes of the first builders ; at
the back was a garden in which nothing
grew, and beyond this was a row of brick
houses of the same date as that in
which Willie Lambton dwelt. Clamber-
ing and clustering against their walls was
an ancient fig-tree. It was the only
green thing that was visible from Willie's
windows, and it was grateful. The fig
was a favourite with our ancestors in

town and country alike; it was succeeded on our walls by the laburnum, and now the creeping wisteria has supplanted both.

Here the sparrows, those strange denizens of the London courts made their home.—Twit-twit! twit-twit! With all the world of wood and meadow open to them, they prefer the close London lanes and alleys. It is contiguity they seek; it is the society of their fellows that compensates for the rest.

And there are men and women, too— more, perhaps, than care to confess it— who prefer the chirp of the sparrows, even in the dog-days, to the music of the grove; men and women that fear to be left alone with their thoughts, it may be, to be cut off from that 'first of joys'— society; men and women who are not only social by habit, but more than commonly gregarious.

In this quaint eyrie Willie Lambton passed most of his time—he rarely returned thither from the crowded saloons or the busy streets without a sensation of relief and of rest. He was soon buried in his books once more, and the whirl of the world passed him by.

With Lemuel, on the contrary, the solitude of his chamber was but preparation for action. He loved to be alone; indeed, he knew no better society than that of his own thoughts, but he yearned for work. To men who have much to accomplish in this world, he would say, time is the most precious of possessions, and they should grudge any portion of it that is not actively employed.

We must hasten onwards. The wise do not look back : it is one of the secrets of success. It depends upon the pace whether, on reaching the summit, we are to sit down and take our ease, and revel in the rarefied air till our ears tingle, and gaze around us at leisure on the transcendent prospect ; or whether we shall discover, to our sorrow, that our labour has been in vain, and that the night is settling down already and dark-ling all round the horizon. They whom death overtakes on attaining the pinnacle of their ambition are its dupes ; they have been cajoled and led on, and en-ticed and cheated ; they have foregone the sweet and pleasant things of life and its ease and its peace for a chimera. It is too late, and they know it ; and when they

upbraid not Heaven, men call it resigna-
tion, and their memories, perchance, are
held in benediction.   But they realise,
nevertheless, with unspeakable bitterness,
the meaning of the melancholy sentence
that every school-boy learns with his
exercise,—

'Seret Agricola arbores quarum fructus
ipse nunquam videbit.'

It happens every day, however; and
some men call it evil fortune, and some
a judgment, and they quarrel over it;
and while they wrangle, time is still
flying over their heads.   Heavens! as
if it mattered, when death is the result
either way!   Call it what ye will, O
my friends!

But Lemuel had the consciousness of
vitality within him; he had the confi-

dence born of innate vigour that is the appanage of the strong. 'Accident excepted, time will befriend me,' was the thought in Lemuel's mind. 'Men will fall on my right hand and on my left, even a second, perchance a third genera- tion, and I shall see them out. With a seven-leagued step I shall pass them by: I am good for eighty!'

CHAPTER XII.

IT was half-past four in the afternoon, and the sun was shining brightly when Daphne returned from her drive to her house in St James's. She drew down hastily the pink blinds, and a delicious glow of warm colour pervaded the room. It was Daphne's favourite tint; it became her amazingly, she believed, and presently her tea-table was spread, and she set herself to preside over it, according to her custom.

It is a veritable hour of witchery. From north and south, east and west, come the trooping athletes of anecdote, and they gather round and close in, like witches over a cauldron. Each has brought something to add to the incantation; and, as the fumes arise, voices grow louder, and the sounds of merriment increase, and the scandal commenced in a whisper ends in a shout.

To command the suffrages of the tea-table would be an object worthy the ambition even of statesmen; but it is a constituency that it is difficult to woo, and that only few men can win. It is at once too exclusive and too wanton. From house to house fly the fair-weather friends, to praise or to censure, to commend or to sneer, as the humour or the caprice of the hour dictates. And woe to the luckless ones whom it is the fashion to decry. Neither man nor woman that has transgressed the code shall escape the lash ; they will be hustled from one to another—no man will take them for his own ; and if the sitting be prolonged, they will scarce survive the daggers of their friends.

Daphne had hardly settled in her chair when the door flew open, and in an instant Bonnie Beauclerc had thrown herself into her arms.

'I am so rejoiced to find you at home,' exclaimed Bonnie, 'for I have something to say which will amuse you. Does it surprise you to hear that I have an admirer ?'

'An admirer! Not in the least, my dearest,' replied Daphne, embracing Bonnie with affection as she said so:

'you know how deeply I have at heart your interests. You must tell me everything; there must be nothing kept back.'

Bonnie's only response was a ringing laugh.

'I am at a loss to comprehend your meaning,' said Daphne, who was beginning to feel a little hurt; 'you must really explain.'

'Then you shall not remain in suspense,' said Bonnie, 'for, indeed, the creature is not worth a second thought, and you will say so when you know it is only that ridiculous Willie Lambton who fancies he has fallen in love with me.'

'Willie Lambton!' repeated Daphne in a tone that indicated surprise; 'you are mistaken surely. Poor, weakly, nerveless

creature ! It is incredible. What im-
aginations you girls have ! I protest
there is not a man in the town that
looks at you awry but you assume forthwith that he is enamoured.'

'Oh, but I can assure you that this is
no mistake,' Bonnie replied. 'Indeed, I
have the utmost difficulty in escaping
from his attentions at the balls. He
pursues me round and round ; he impor-
tunes me to dance ; he entreats me to sup ;
if I smile he is in an ecstasy; if I am serious
his face lengthens and he is in despair.'

Here Bonnie illustrated her narrative
by a corresponding grimace, which drew
from Daphne repeated peals of laughter.
Their merriment was still at its height,
when it was interrupted by the entry of
Miniver Green.

'My dear Lady Beauport,' Miniver exclaimed, 'complete my good fortune in finding you thus pleasantly engaged by admitting me to the secrets of the tea-table. There are none more delightful in my estimation—absolutely none.'

Miniver's speech did but add to the hilarity of Daphne and her cousin.

'It is nothing,' cried Daphne when she had recovered sufficiently the use of articulate language; 'it is really nothing at all; quite too silly, at least, to bear repetition.'

'At this hour the more silly the more acceptable,' said Miniver. 'We have disposed of the business of the day; we have been sad and serious, and nature calls aloud for a contrast. Even a philosopher may be flippant over his tea-cup.'

'Well, if you insist upon knowing,' said Daphne.

'I am inexorable,' interrupted Miniver —'adamantine.'

'Then you must know that Bonnie has been describing the attentions of her latest admirer. You would hardly expect to find him in the person of Marcia Mowbray's young brother, Willie Lambton?'

'I am not astonished in the least to hear you say so,' said Miniver with an assumption of gravity, 'for I have observed that your sentimental man is perpetually on the point of making love. Sentiment wanders vaguely in the air, is diffused throughout space until, gathered together and concentrated by some subtle influence, or fortuitous concourse, it is condensed of a sudden and falls to the

earth in the concrete form of love. Your
sentimental man becomes forthwith the
ready medium of its action, and thenceforth the process is quite regular. Love,
once it has begun to operate, follows well
ascertained laws; and in this instance it
would seem that the young man has
passed through the preliminary stages
with commendable exactness. For myself I detest your skirmishers,' Miniver
added, 'your irregulars; I am a man of
order, and predisposed in favour of
him whose approaches are made in due
form.'

Miniver Green delivered himself of
these oracular sentences with an air of
affected solemnity, his head slightly ele-
vated and one hand extended, while with
the other he grasped his tea-cup.

'You appear to contemplate one side of the case only,' said Daphne, 'that of the man; and this may be natural enough from your point of view; but pray take some account of the lady's position. It may be that the man's sentiment, or love, if you will, is not reciprocated, and his approaches, as you term them, may, in that case, end in persecution.'

'That is, no doubt, a conceivable contingency,' said Miniver; 'but the persecution that is born of love is surely one of the beatitudes? You cannot find it in your heart to be angry with the Despot of the ball-room, or to execrate the Diocletian of the boudoir?'

'Well, not angry exactly,' said Bonnie Beauclerc, laughing, 'that would be too

strong a word, perhaps; but then, Willie
Lambton is often provokingly in the way.
To be sure, when I send him to speak
to the footman, or to call the carriage,
he is delighted, poor man!'

'Poor man!' echoed Miniver, as he
relinquished his cup and sought his snuff-
box. 'Alas! poor man.'

And Bonnie had indeed spoken the
truth; for Willie Lambton had fallen
madly in love with the beautiful girl.
He raved about her, and at times tried
to think that his love was returned. It
was the only passion that had ever stirred
his heart to its depths, and it took possession of him entirely. But Bonnie
played with Willie Lambton as with a
shuttlecock. She tossed him in the air
and turned him round and round, and

laughed in his face when she had made
him giddy. He groaned in spirit, and
she skipped lightly; he was heart-sick,
and her merriment became boisterous.
Bonnie Beauclerc knew nothing of abstract
affections—of love in the air she understood as little as of love in a cottage.
Love, or what passed for it, was never
dissociated in her mind from the possession of wealth and station, and Willie
Lambton was painfully conscious of his
inability to confer either. He sought
to persuade himself, however, that his
affection would be no more slighted were
the fatal obstacle removed; and this motive acted thenceforth as a spur urging
him perpetually to effort. From supine
indifference he became even nervously
energetic; he toiled without ceasing, and

waited no longer in expectation of briefs that seldom or never came to his door. In the highways he sought them, and at the dawn he might be found labouring still at the work he had collected during the previous day. Poor Willie Lambton! day by day his pale features grew paler · still, his brow more troubled, as the anxious days passed on and the feverish nights, and but little progress was made towards realising a fortune.

The marriage of Sanctimonious Stanhope and Egidia Mowbray had been the sensation of the early season, and society tittered and twittered over it. Society was amused, and its curiosity was excited by the violence of the experiment and the flagrancy of the contrast. No man permitted himself to think that a marriage contracted under such conditions could be otherwise than disastrous. The interesting question was how long the marriage tie would bear the strain to which it was subjected. But Stanhope was jubilant, for he was of the number of those 'who listen with credulity to the whispers of fancy, and pursue with eagerness the phantoms of hope; who think that age will fulfil the promises of youth, and the deficiencies of the present day be supplied by the morrow.'

The joy-bells rang out merrily; there was no strain of sadness or of warning in them; but for Stanhope, as for most men whose fancy has outrun their reason, there came a time when he too shared the experiences of Rasselas, Prince of Abyssinia.

In an instant, it may be, in the twinkling of an eye, the fantastic illusions vanish, perish away, and almost precipitately disappear. The fond dreams dissolve, and it is found that the order of nature has not been reversed or set aside after all ; that the sun sets at the appointed hour, and men proceed to light their lamps.

To most men the illusions of life come early ; the laughter of to-day is succeeded by the tears of the morrow, and for an hour the storm rages furiously. But it does not last, for the youthful mind is not prone to grieve, and thereafter comes ripe experience, that leads on to tranquil and mellow age. It is otherwise, however, with the illusions of advanced life. They do not melt ; they harden with time, and the gloom gathers as they cast back their melancholy shadows that darken all the landscape.

Soon the midnight oil commenced to burn freely in the mansion over which Egidia was called to preside in Grosvenor Square ; the door was ever ajar, and the gay spirits of the town quickly recognised that another house had been added to the list of those which were after their own heart. Night after night the sounds of revelry arose, and the tables were spread with the rare and delicate viands that render the entertainments of the early spring the most delightful of the year. Night after night the light chords were struck, and the sounding bass made music for the corybantes of the ballroom, and longer and longer grew the face of

Sanctimonious Stanhope as the hours of repose grew shorter and the night ceased to be distinguished from the day by any line sharply drawn.

But the revellers were not abashed, for Egidia herself it was that led the way and cheered them on. During ten long years had she waited for this chance, and now that she had obtained her freedom, was she to be expected to forego it ?

'I have fulfilled my contract,' Egidia would say. 'I have married a man whose habits are not mine, it is true, but it gratified him, and shall not I, too, have a reward ? I am no recluse,' she would reply to the querulous remonstrances of her husband. 'My inclinations do not tend that way; my enjoyment is in the world around me—this fair and joyous world—and the living, not the dead, shall be my associates.'

To argue the case was idle. Sanctimonious Stanhope found that Egidia was inexorable, and when he complained to his friends there was no reply. They would smile and evade the question, or pass flippantly on their way.

'I don't know a man that is more miserable than Stanhope,' observed Miniver Green, as he walked away from Grosvenor Square at the dawn of a summer morning. 'It was but yesterday, it seems to me, that I envied his position. To-day I believe he would gladly take mine. Dear me! marriage is a serious matter.'

'It is not marriage that is to blame,' said Lemuel; 'it is the abuse of it. Had not Stanhope postponed marriage till now, when such a venture is perilous, he might have married more than once and been the better for it. As it is, he has challenged fate, and sent the hostile message by Cupid; he must be prepared for the consequences of his folly.'

'It is futile, or worse, to argue with sentiment,' said Miniver, 'or to philosophise over love; in nine cases out of ten sentiment prevails over reason, and hence flow evils as desolating as any that escaped from Pandora's box to afflict mankind. Nay, the case is worse still, it seems to me; for not even hope remains behind to console suffering humanity.'

'True,' Lemuel remarked; 'but I do not confound love with marriage. Love is an abstract thing and intangible, that may be dismissed after a trial, but marriage is pre-eminently concrete.'

'There is indeed no questioning its realities,' Miniver replied, 'and to me it has appeared that they are not unfitly heralded by the awe-inspiring ceremonies of the marriage day. If women were wise, surely they would simplify the ritual; as it now stands, many a man shies at the programme, even if he do not bolt outright.'

'The trial may be severe in compliance with the exigencies of fashion,' remarked Lemuel, 'but I do not concur as to its deterrent effects. It must be confessed that the man who thus counts and forecasts is not in love. A lover's self-control I can understand, for it is the instinct of self-preservation; the

interests at stake may be gigantic, overwhelming ; but the lover that uses the
microscope is an enigma to the gods, and
a spectacle that should suffice to make just
men weep.'

CHAPTER XIII.

AS the season advanced rumours affecting the stability of the Government gained circulation, and the House of Commons was permeated by the undefinable instinct that precedes the downfall of a Ministry. Party discipline becomes relaxed; the ranks are broken and men fall out; the whips themselves partake of the all but universal loosening of party ties, and the House assumes a straggling and dissipated appearance that nothing short of a dissolution can cure. Even sober men begin to speak with a reckless air at such a time, and Ministers to stammer; they have no heart for eloquence,—the words stick in the throat. The House loses its self-confidence; it is conscious that its credit with the country is shaken, that it is capable no longer of compassing great measures. The contagion spreads to the provinces; the constituencies are quickly alive to the fact that a blight has fallen on the assembly, and soon are made manifest the excitement and clamour of the coming election.

'I parted with Nestor in the Mall not half-an-hour since,' said James Mowbray, on meeting Miniver Green at the club. 'He tells me that things are looking serious. He is in the confidence of Ministers, you know, and I am disposed to credit what he says, for, though men in office, or seeking it, may speak for a purpose, pensioners for life will often tell the truth.'

'Nestor having ceased to belong to the Cabinet, may not be sorry to see the Government in trouble, Miniver maintained; he is devoured by vanity, and that the fall of the Ministry, now that he has left it, would be welcomed by him with a secret satisfaction there can be little doubt. For myself, I think that his anticipations are somewhat exaggerated.'

'It may be so,' said Mowbray; 'but the impression gains ground that the state of Ireland, coupled with the advance of democracy, will lead to the downfall of the Government.'

'The state of Ireland!' exclaimed Miniver; 'why, if the state of Ireland were to be the test, no Government could hold office for a week. It is the conundrum of every Cabinet.'

'The fact is,' said Mowbray, 'that each Government falls into the same groove as its predecessor, so far as Irish policy is concerned; they don't know the country with which they have to deal, and the people on our side of the House are not less ignorant in this respect than their opponents. In my opinion, a man should be required to serve an apprenticeship under indenture of three years at the least in Ireland before he is deemed eligible for a seat in the Cabinet.'

'But Irishmen are not agreed among themselves,' said Miniver, 'as to what is best for their country. They contradict each other freely, and that is, to my mind, the disheartening feature. We in England seek to humour both parties, and in so doing share not infrequently the traditional fate of those who rest upon two stools.'

' True, Irishmen contradict each other,' said Mowbray ; ' and this adds immeasurably to the difficulties of Englishmen in the matter of legislation ; but Irishmen have at least decided views, and in England we have not yet attained that stage. Events move rapidly, however, and, unless the Government decide on a vigorous line of action, it will fall. The Irish, at home and abroad, are not to be trifled with ; say what you will, they have grown into a great nation, even if you be not disposed to admit that they are a wise and an understanding people.'

'They would be formidable, indeed, if united,' said Miniver; 'but their power is broken to pieces by intestine quarrels.'

'Their fierce contentions have, it is true, made them powerless for great purposes,' Mowbray observed; 'but the Irish fight, they do not quarrel: it is, so far, a fine trait in the national character.'

'I think the correction is just,' Miniver replied, 'though the circumstance does not, I apprehend, improve the aspect of the case. I wonder whether Beauport is prepared with a policy?'

'Beauport is mostly at Newmarket,' said Mowbray; 'and the atmosphere of the place is not congenial to the inception of political action. True, Beauport is the only member of the Government who, to my mind, is a man of genius; but, if he were to devote more of his time to his office, and less to the race-course, it would be all the better for his reputation.'

'I am not altogether satisfied of that,' Miniver replied; 'a sporting minister is ever a popular minister; the people in this country come to understand a racing man and to take an interest in him. It is the next thing to believing in him, and that will follow with a little management.'

'For myself,' said Mowbray, 'I should as soon place faith in a gambling attorney as in a racing minister. Thank heaven! I belong to a serious party, one that is ever conscious of the responsibilities of government.'

'A party that is persistently serious,' said Miniver, 'betrays distrust of its powers. It labours at the task before it with an anxious mind that leaves no breathing time ; it trudges along the dusty road driven by whips and goads, nor ever turns into the green glades by the way-side for recreation or repose. Such men are liable to be worn out prematurely. They, on the other hand, that laugh and sing as they labour, show themselves masters of the situation, and inspire confidence. A statesman should not be frivolous, I admit, but he has to manipulate mankind, and for this end a jest is often a better argument than a syllogism. It is so in the House of Commons. The man that makes the best jest in the best taste is ever the most successful, as he is the most acceptable speaker. We are a laughter-loving people, and the cap and bells are seldom absent long from the buskin. By the way, Leverson dines with us this evening,—will you be of the party ? '

' With all my heart,' Miniver replied. ' I regard Leverson as one of the rising young men of the day, and his companionship has for me, I confess, an abiding interest. We old fellows, tottering to our fall, may see in promising youth a prophecy as well as a guarantee of the future. We can look a-head in their company and gain a glimpse, at least, of the world that will follow after us. Leverson is an excellent specimen of his class, and a capital talker, too, when he is in the humour.'

' Of the two, I admire his silence the more,' said Mowbray ; ' it seems to me to be the more artistic, the more finished performance, and, strange to say, even the more eloquent. It is more significant

than words that are not intended to convey any meaning.　But I cannot convince
my wife of this, for Leverson has contrived
to array the women on his side, and they
stand together like the Theban Band.'

'Then he need not despair of being
Prime Minister some day,' said Miniver;
'for the influence of the women is a power
that has to be reckoned with even in politics: it confronts you at every turn, and
will go a long way towards inclining the
balance in your favour.　It is a lever in
public life, the value of which is best
known to the wise: the politician that is
patronised by the women is already on
the way to Downing Street.'

During dinner Lemuel was unusually
cheerful.　For the moment he appeared
to have thrown aside some of the reserve

that was habitual with him, and his conversation was brilliant and animated.

Marcia Mowbray was at a loss to find an explanation of the change; she had observed keenly every symptom that helped to throw light upon the prospects of the Government, and they were uniformly adverse. She looked forward eagerly to its downfall, and the consequent return to office of her husband, and at the present crisis it was inexplicable that Lemuel, connected as he was with the Ministry, should display only indications of rejoicing. 'Is his manner to-night but a blind,' thought Marcia, 'assumed to conceal his chagrin? or—is he in love?'

It is ever the alternative of a woman's difficulty; to her everything revolves round this central sun of her existence;

and she has recourse to it for the explanation of whatever is strange or unexpected. Marcia Mowbray watched Lemuel with some of the interest with which astronomers are wont to observe the motions of a meteor whose course is noticed to be erratic. They are convinced that it follows a law, and that its movements are not haphazard; it would be a scandal to science to suppose it were otherwise, and theory after theory is started to account for the phenomenon, but fails to satisfy altogether. Lemuel was not a man to fall in love, Marcia knew; it was the last thing she would have predicted of him, and it was only in despair of discovering any more probable motive that she hazarded the conjecture. Her eyes were fastened upon him; but it was a mask that she beheld,—

there was no penetrating it, and ever and anon the question rose to her lips : who can she be ?

To Willie Lambton it was that Marcia turned for information ; for, if Lemuel had a friend to whom more than to another he would be likely to unbosom himself, that man was Willie Lambton. But Willie only smiled when Marcia propounded her theory.

' Lemuel in love ! Impossible. Why, for him the word has no meaning.'

' I suppose a man might contemplate marriage, however, without being in love exactly,' observed Marcia, who was unwilling to surrender her position altogether, — ' to satisfy his ambition for example, or to promote it ?'

' Well, I suppose he might,' Willie replied sadly; 'but what a dreary future he would have before him! Only to think of marriage without love! It would surely be better in such a case for a man not to marry at all?'

'I am not so sure of that,' said Marcia; 'it would depend very much upon the individual. Some men are said to have no feelings, and you would, it seems, include Lemuel Leverson in the number; but the term is only comparative at the most, and even that qualification may be too strong. In some men sentiment is concentrated, and its intensity makes itself manifest immediately; in others it is spread over a greater surface it may be, but the amount is much the same in the end. No; the difference is in most cases not nearly so great as you seem to imagine : it is surprising how much alike one man is to another when once you have discounted the cut of his coat.'

'It may be even so,' said Willie, 'though I find a difficulty, I confess, in understanding these placid natures—these philandering philosophers. For myself, I think I should prefer being emancipated from sentiment altogether, rather than have it doled out to me in such scant measures. To me it has always seemed that Lemuel has no feelings, only principles.'

'You mean virtues?' inquired Marcia.

'Not exactly. Principles are the fruit of judgment, as virtues are of religion. Lemuel's actions are regulated by principles dictated by judgment, principles of honour, principles of expediency, it may be. Virtue is more rigid and less selfish.'

'You know him better than I do,' said Marcia, 'and I will not, therefore, dispute your opinion. Perhaps, then, you can explain the change that has come over him to-night, now that you are satisfied that it is not to be attributed to love.'

'To you it may seem otherwise,' said Willie Lambton; 'but, nevertheless, I am convinced that it is to politics that we must look for an explanation. Politics alone are the mainspring of Lemuel's actions. To succeed in political life is his settled aim and purpose; and if you would fathom his motives, you must accept this as a fundamental axiom.'

Marcia Mowbray remained incredulous,

however, for she was unable to recon-
cile this theory with the indications presented. She was still engaged in turning
over in her mind the contradictions
involved in it, when the door opened,
and Nestor was ushered into her presence. Nestor was flurried.

'On my way hither I met Beauport,'
Nestor explained. 'He is much concerned for the fate of the Ministry. The
crisis is acute, he declared—is desperate,
in short. The revolution has broken
out.'

'The revolution!' exclaimed half-a-
dozen voices in chorus. 'But where?'

'In the House of Commons.'

END OF VOL. I.

COLSTON AND SON, PRINTERS, EDINBURGH.